The Call
of the Wild

ANNOTATED AND ILLUSTRATED

The Call of the Wild

ANNOTATED AND ILLUSTRATED

By
Jack London

Edited by
Daniel Dyer

UNIVERSITY OF OKLAHOMA PRESS
Norman

Also edited by Daniel Dyer
Jack London, *The Call of the Wild,*
with an Illustrated Reader's Companion (Norman, 1995)

Library of Congress Cataloging-in-Publication Data

London, Jack, 1876-1916.
The call of the wild / Jack London.
—Annotated and illustrated / edited by Daniel Dyer.
p.   cm.
Includes bibliographical references.
ISBN 978-0-8061-2920-4 (alk. paper)
1. London, Jack, 1876-1916. Call of the wild.
2. Klondike River Valley (Yukon)—Gold discoveries—Fiction.
3. Klondike River Valley (Yukon)—In literature.
4. Dogs—Klondike River Valley (Yukon)—Fiction.
5. Dogs in literature.
I. Dyer, Daniel (Daniel Osborn), 1944-
II. Title.
PS3523.046C3   1997
818'.52—dc20
96-42010
CIP

The paper in this book meets the guidelines for permanence
and durability of the Committee on Production Guidelines for Book Longevity
of the Council on Library Resources, Inc. ∞

For my son,
Stephen Osborn Dyer,
who has shared the adventure.

Contents

Foreword

ON DECEMBER 1, 1902, Jack London began writing a short story that would "get away" from him and grow to become the novel *The Call of the Wild*. He had just returned from England, where his nonfiction work *The People of the Abyss* had captured with youthful passion and indignation the abject poverty of life in the East End of the city of London. By January 26, 1903, only a few short weeks after beginning *The Call of the Wild*, London submitted the finished manuscript to the *Saturday Evening Post*, where it was immediately accepted for serial publication. Soon thereafter the author mailed his novel to Macmillan Company, the publisher with whom he recently had signed a six-book contract on the strength of his Klondike short stories.

So began the life of one of the most famous and well-loved classic works of American literature. When London wrote the novel, he had no real sense of the importance and destiny of the book he called simply his "dog story." Indeed, his correspondence with George Brett, his editor at Macmillan, shows that, as a young, largely unknown author, he saw himself as a neophyte whose mature, most important efforts still lay before him. After settling on a title for his new novel (*The Wolf* and *The Sleeping Wolf* were candidates until London allowed that *The Call of the Wild* was growing on him), he wrote to Brett on March 25, 1903: "I cannot convey to you the greatness of my pleasure at knowing that the book has struck you favorably; for I feel, therefore, that it is an earnest of the work I hope to do for you when I find myself. And find myself I will, some day." London would produce many more works that would bear out his confident prediction, but he did not realize at this point that he had already found himself and begun to fulfill his authorial promise. He had already written his most famous work, the one on which his reputation would chiefly rest for most of his readers.

The Call of the Wild immediately became a bestseller, and it established Jack London's fame throughout the world. It rapidly attained the status of a literary classic, a timeless story with universal appeal and meaning. From its first publication in 1903 it has never been out of print, an astonishing achievement, and it has been translated into scores of languages, helping to make London the most popular American author outside the United States. A look at the shelves of any library or bookstore reveals many editions, each offering its own attractions to readers. Among all these editions, Daniel Dyer's stands out, for his fine introduction, and for the maps, historic photographs, and extensive annotations that contextualize the novel's content for readers.

For students and teachers, as well as for anyone who simply enjoys reading a tale well-told, Dyer's mining of the historical context of the novel yields rich nuggets of information to enrich all readers' enjoyment and understanding. The maps, for example, reveal the geography of the Klondike and the locations of its towns, lakes, mountains, and other landmarks—enabling the reader to visualize the distances and terrain traveled by dog teams. The notes likewise support a full appreciation of the novel, explaining local, archaic, and Indian words as used by the characters and showing how London used historic events and practices to provide authenticity in his narrative of the harsh life in the frozen Northland.

Whether one reads *The Call of the Wild* simply for its story or for deeper meaning at multiple levels, it is an enduring classic because, as Dyer points out in his introduction, it ignites the imagination as it informs the heart. Like the novel itself, Daniel Dyer's edition will live on as a classic, to be read and reread by generations of Jack London students, scholars, and fans.

Sara S. Hodson
Curator of Literary Manuscripts
Huntington Library

Preface

WHEN JACK LONDON wrote the final words to *The Call of the Wild* in January 1903, he could not have imagined that what he modestly called "my dog story" would one day become one of the most popular books in the world. And yet it has. The volume can now be found in scores of languages and in dozens of versions. Millions of copies of the book have been published. There have been movies, cartoons, and comic books retelling the adventures of Buck.

However, in some ways the book has become increasingly inaccessible to new generations of readers. In late 1902, when London began writing his tale of the Klondike Gold Rush, he was confident that most of his readers were familiar with its historical and geographical aspects. The Rush, which had ended in 1899, was still fresh in the public mind. Tens of thousands of persons had left home for the Klondike, and for many months feature stories on the Rush and the region had appeared in most major magazines of the day. Some of the larger newspapers had for weeks devoted entire sections to Klondike coverage.

But now, a century later, few people other than historians—or residents of the Yukon— know much about the facts of the Gold Rush. Fewer still are familiar with the geography of the Northland. Or with the techniques of travel by dog team. Or with Jack London's own experiences in California and the Yukon, many of which figure prominently in the tale. Accordingly, many of today's readers of London's novel are at a disadvantage, for, without the background that the book assumes, they are simply unable to see what London saw—and in many cases *remembered*—as he composed the novel.

Until very recently there has been no edition of the book that explained fully the historical, geographical, biographical, and social aspects of the story; there has been no edition with detailed maps and photographs from the Gold Rush era. In 1995, however, the University of Oklahoma Press published my *The Call of the Wild, with an Illustrated Reader's Companion,* an edition intended for literary scholars and historians. Now, the present volume will be the most completely annotated edition available to general readers and students.

Text

No manuscript or typed version of *The Call of the Wild* exists. It is probable that London, who had no reason to expect that his novel would become a fixed star in America's literary firmament, simply discarded his notes and manuscript copies once the book was published. Neither the *Saturday Evening Post,* which first serialized the story, nor Macmillan, first publisher of the book, has retained in its archives London's original typescript.

Accordingly, I have elected to reproduce here the first edition published by the Macmillan Company in July 1903, retaining all of London's original spelling and punctuation. London read page proofs for this edition, so we can be confident that it is close to what he had originally written and intended. The version of the novel that appeared in the *Saturday Evening Post* in five installments between 20 June and 18 July 1903 differs considerably from the book. Chapter divisions are different, and—most significantly—the bulk of Chapter 6 is missing. When the *Post* editors asked London to cut five thousand words, he accommodated them by chopping out some of the best-known episodes in the novel: the near-tragedy on the cliff, the attack on "Black" Burton, the rescue of John Thornton in the rapids, and the wager on Buck's pulling the thousand-pound sled load.

Annotations

In the endnotes I have addressed such subjects as the following:

Geography. London mentions many place-names in the text. Every one is actual. Every one can be pinpointed on the maps accompanying this edition. For each place I have provided a brief description and, when appropriate, explained the origin of the name. Although I have retained London's spellings in his text and on the maps, I have used in my notes the standard spellings of today.

Public Transportation. In chapter 1, Buck travels by rail, ferry, and steamship. Using published timetables from 1897, I have been able to determine the actual routes Buck would have taken.

Autobiography. In this—as in other stories—London drew upon his own experiences in California and the Klondike. I have, where confidence and common sense permit, pointed out events with autobiographical significance.

Personal Names. Jack London sprinkled the names of family, friends, acquaintances, and historical figures throughout his fiction.

History. Throughout, I have explained allusions to actual historical events.

Language. Where possible, I have defined the slang, American Indian words, and other unfamiliar locutions London employs.

Dogs and Travel by Dogsled. I have provided information about unfamiliar breeds of dogs and about the techniques of travel by dogsled.

Flora and Fauna. London was scrupulously accurate about the plants and animals he mentioned in the story. Accordingly, I have said little about such subjects—except for species of unusual significance or obscurity.

I have of course explained London's allusions to various items (for example, Pullman cars and Hudson's Bay Company firearms) that are no longer part of our common knowledge.

The Bibliography

In the bibliography I have listed London's other Northland writing, the major biographies, major criticism of *The Call of the Wild*, the most significant general histories and personal accounts of the Klondike Gold Rush, and some general references. For a more comprehensive list, see Jack London, *The Call of the Wild, with an Illustrated Reader's Companion,* edited by Daniel Dyer (University of Oklahoma Press, 1995).

To prepare this volume and the more comprehensive annotated edition, I visited and corresponded with libraries, archives, historical societies, and historians all over the country. I thank them all as I did in my earlier edition.

I do wish to acknowledge here, however, the assistance of the National Endowment for the Humanities. In 1990 I participated in a NEH Summer Seminar ("Jack London: The Major Works") where I began the work on this project under the guidance and encouragement of Earle Labor; in 1992–93 I was a recipient of the NEH–*Reader's Digest* Teacher-Scholar Award, a year-long sabbatical grant that enabled me to complete virtually all of the research for these editions.

Also, I wish to express my gratitude to I. Milo Shepard, who, as great-nephew of Jack London and executor of the Trust of Irving Shepard and London's literary estate, granted me access to London materials at the Huntington Library, San Marino, California. Librarians at the Huntington and at the Newberry Library have been especially helpful throughout the course of my work.

The late Russ Kingman provided much information and even more encouragement over the years. His death removed from the world a wonderful human being and an irreplaceable resource for London scholars. His wife, Winnie, remains a loyal friend and peerless source of materials and advice.

My editors at the University of Oklahoma Press—Kim Wiar, Sarah Nestor, and Sarah Iselin—have throughout my relationship with the Press exhibited that rare combination of competence, compassion, and a fierce determination to get things right. I am grateful for their remarkable efforts—and for my good fortune in finding them.

Finally, I thank my scattered family, who, from their various residences on both coasts, sustained me in every imaginable way. My wife, Joyce, as always, has been my finest critic and most devoted supporter.

DANIEL DYER

Introduction

IN JULY 1898, when Jack London, aged twenty-two, sick with scurvy and virtually penniless, returned home to Oakland, California, from the Klondike, he discovered that his stepfather, John London, had died. He would now have to find a way to support his mother, Flora, and his nephew, Johnny Miller.

Before departing for the Klondike, London had been spectacularly unsuccessful as a writer. He had composed scores of pieces—stories, articles, plays, even poems and jokes—and publishers had summarily rejected them all. Back from the North, he continued to suffer ill fortune on into the fall of 1898: he mailed away his writing; it came back in his return envelope. Later, in his autobiographical novel *Martin Eden,* he described his frustrations with this impersonal process:

> There was no human editor at the other end, but a mere cunning arrangement of cogs that changed the manuscript from one envelope to another and stuck on the stamps. It was like the slot machines.... It depended upon which slot one dropped the penny in, whether he got chocolate or gum. And so with the editorial machine. One slot brought checks and the other brought rejection slips. So far he had found only the latter slot.

In October 1898, desperate, he took a Civil Service examination to qualify for a job in the post office. In mid-January 1899 he learned that he had won an appointment as a mail carrier and was prepared to accept the position. But his mother urged him to continue with his writing, and so he turned down the job and returned to his lonely work. Success soon followed. The world had become as curious about the Northland as London was eager to explain it. Before the year was out, his stories appeared in the *Overland Monthly, Youth's Companion,* and *Atlantic Monthly.* He signed a contract with Houghton Mifflin for *The Son of the Wolf,* his first collection of Klondike stories. He had finally found the other slot.

Four years later, London finished *The Call of the Wild,* the novel that would propel him into international literary celebrity. He wrote the entire book in two months, but could not decide on a title. He suggested, then withdrew, *The Sleeping Wolf* (which would appear a few years later as a chapter title in *White Fang*). *The Wolf* was yet another idea. He argued for *The Call of the Wild* instead of *Call of the Wild.* Finally—although he admitted in a letter that he "did not like the title"—he grudgingly accepted *The Call of the Wild.* Then he sold all serial rights to the *Saturday Evening Post* for $750 and all book rights to the Macmillan Company for $2,000. He would never receive one cent more for this, his bestselling book.

On 17 August 1896, George Washington Carmack and two American Indian companions, Tagish Charley and Skookum Jim Mason, were prospecting the tributaries of the Klondike River, which is itself a tributary of the Yukon River. On Rabbit Creek—soon to be renamed Bonanza—they made a massive gold discovery that would trigger the last great American gold rush.

As word of Carmack's strike spread throughout the remote mining camps of the Yukon and Alaska, prospectors abandoned their claims and headed for the mouth of the Klondike River. A trickle of men quickly became a stream, and soon every creek in the region was staked and claimed, mouth to source.

On 16 July 1897—nearly a year after the initial strike—the steamship *Excelsior,* loaded with gold and prospectors with tales to tell, docked in San Francisco; a day later the *Portland,* similarly loaded, arrived in Seattle. Newspapers trumpeted the discovery, which was exciting news to a country in the throes of an economic downturn. And the northward stream of humanity became a raging torrent. In his stunning history, *Klondike: The Last Great Gold Rush, 1896–1899,* Pierre Berton wrote that one million people made plans to go to the Yukon, one hundred thousand actually set out, and thirty thousand actually reached Dawson City, the boom town that sprang up at the mouth of the Klondike.

The northward journey was one of breath-taking beauty, enormous expense, and heartbreaking difficulty. Although there were a number of routes attempted throughout the Rush, the principal one—and the one that figures in *The Call of the Wild*—required travellers to take a steamer to one of two neighboring towns on the southeastern coast of Alaska, Skagway and Dyea. Both towns—about nine miles apart by a winding road—sat at the foot of the Coast Mountains and served as staging areas for the assault on one of two formidable alpine passes. From Skagway, the gold seekers ascended the White Pass, a trail so severe and unforgiving that it soon earned another name—the Dead Horse Trail. No pack animal survived it the first winter, not until George Brackett completed his wagon road to the summit in the spring of 1898.

Dyea offered another pass, the Chilkoot, every bit as difficult as the White Pass. The final quarter-mile of the Chilkoot is a forty-five degree incline that required the argonauts—as the gold seekers were called in the press—to hack stairs into the ice during that brutal winter of 1897–98 when seventy feet of snow fell at the summit. "The Golden Stairs," they were called.

At the summit of both passes travellers left Alaska and entered British Columbia. At their mountaintop posts the North-west Mounted Police—the law in the Canadian North—collected customs duties and turned back all persons without a year's supplies—death was certain without them. Accordingly, prospectors needed to make repeated trips to the summit—sometimes as many as fifty—in order to transport their ton of goods.

From the summit of the Coast Mountains hundreds of miles stretched between the argonauts and the gold. About seventeen miles away, however, were two lakes, Lindeman and Bennett—headwaters of the Yukon River—where the gold seekers cut down every tree for miles around to construct boats to carry them the remaining five hundred miles downriver to Dawson City.

On 29 May 1898 the ice finally broke in the lakes, and seven thousand boats set sail, producing what must have been one of the most spectacular sights in the history of human folly. The Yukon River, which proceeds at a brisk nine knots its entire length, offered several deadly challenges to the argonauts, most of whom were inexperienced navigators and sailors. The first was Miles (or Box) Canyon, a spot where the Yukon River narrowed sharply as its enormous volume of water was channelled between rocky cliffs that at some places rose 100 feet above the surface. Boats shot through the canyon like rockets. Some crashed horribly into the rocks, or were caught in whirlpools. In his diary my great-grandfather noted how water flew over his head during his spectacular ride through Miles in 1898.

Just beyond the canyon were the Whitehorse and Squaw Rapids, which in the first days claimed fifteen hundred boats and five lives. The North-west Mounted Police quickly took charge at the rapids and permitted only experienced white-water navigators to attempt the Whitehorse. Others had to portage their goods and craft.

About 220 miles farther downriver were the Five Finger Rapids—huge rocks that bulged up out of the water and smashed any craft that did not stay far to the right during the passage. A couple of miles farther were the Rink Rapids, least dangerous of all. Beyond Rink about 230 miles of river remained, but there were no more spots of deadly peril—only an occasional snag or sandbar.

On 8 June 1898 the first wave of crafts reached Dawson City, and the argonauts discovered, to their alarm and disappointment, that all of the claims on all of the creeks had been staked for nearly two years. For the thousands of new arrivals there was only a handful of choices: look for employment on the claims of others, wait for a claim to be abandoned (as my great-grandfather did), practice the trade or craft they thought they had left behind, go to work for the White Pass and Yukon Railroad (which was constructing a rail line over the White Pass from Skagway to Lake Bennett), or try to find the money to pay for a steamboat ticket to St. Michael, nearly two thousand miles away on the western Alaska coast, and a ship for home.

Among the many disappointed thousands was young Jack London. Although he had been one of the first to depart for Alaska (he sailed aboard the *Umatilla* on 25 July 1897, only about a week after news of the strike reached San Francisco), he was unable to reach Dawson City before freeze-up. Like many other thousands, he landed in Dyea, hauled his outfit over the Chilkoot Pass, constructed two boats near Lake Lindeman, and began the float to Dawson. But time and weather were against him. Fierce storms delayed him on Lake Laberge, and the ice in the river was thickening.

On 9 October, London and his party arrived at the mouth of the Stewart River, about seventy miles short of their destination. There they found some abandoned cabins on an island and, uncertain of the availability of lodging in Dawson, decided to spend the winter right where they were. In the early weeks of October, London and his partners staked some claims on nearby Henderson Creek—claim 54 on the left fork of Henderson Creek bears London's signature—but for most of the winter he remained in his cabin, greeting wayfarers of all sorts—North-west Mounted Police, American Indians, dog mushers, mail carriers, and determined gold seekers. From his observations and conversations he filled the storehouse of information that would lend such convincing verisimilitude to his Northland tales.

In May, London began to suffer from scurvy brought on by a diet devoid of fruits and vegetables, and on 8 June 1898 he left Dawson City by boat with two companions, Charles

Taylor and John Thorson. About three weeks later they reached St. Michael, Alaska, and boarded a steamer for home—and in London's case, for fame.

From his year in the Klondike, Jack London fashioned dozens of stories, several novels, and a handful of articles. But in *The Call of the Wild* he compressed the entire sprawling Klondike experience into a spare and poetic thirty-two thousand words. Like his creator, the dog Buck travels from California to Dyea, traverses the Chilkoot Pass, follows the Yukon River trail (the frozen surface of the river was the highway for dog teams), and arrives at Dawson City. Like his creator, Buck nearly dies in the Northland but eventually triumphs, becomes the stuff of legend.

The novel—London's seventh book—enjoyed immediate critical and popular acclaim. "[A] marvelously graphic picture of the great gold rush to the Klondike. . . . Fierce, brutal, splashed with blood, and alive with the crack of whip and blow of club," gushed the *San Francisco Chronicle* (August 1903). "It is the best thing the public has had so far from the pen of a young author who . . . has already shown a fresh and vigorous bent in story," offered the *Athenaeum* (August 1903). "[F]ar and away the best book that Mr. Jack London has ever written," added the *Bookman* (October 1903). "[N]ot a pretty story at all, but a very powerful one," offered the more restrained *Atlantic Monthly* (November 1903).

Modern-day critics have been no less enthusiastic about the novel. Maxwell Geismar (1960) called the novel a "famous fable," "a handsome parable of buried impulses," and "a beautiful prose poem." Franklin Walker (1960) says that it "belongs on a shelf with *Walden* and *Huckleberry Finn*." Earle Labor (1967) describes it as "a poem informed by the rhythms of epic and myth," in which we hear "the faint but clear echo of an inner music." Charles Child Walcutt (1974) calls it London's "purest book"; Rothberg (1981), the "most perfectly realized novel he ever wrote." And E. L. Doctorow (1990) labels it a "mordant parable . . . his masterpiece."

Throughout its life of nearly a century, *The Call of the Wild* has entertained and educated readers on a variety of levels. Its raw narrative power is apparent from the early pages where Buck is stolen by a gardener's helper and finds himself a deposed and imprisoned king aboard a train to San Francisco. Moreover, the novel provides a series of clear, brutal snapshots of life in the North—and of the great Gold Rush that invaded the region. Merciless dogs and men fight to the death. The vast Yukon wilderness destroys those who fail to respect it. Men labor "like giants" to extract riches from the grudging ground.

Some readers have noticed the many threads that connect the lives of Buck and Jack

London. Buck's story begins on a ranch that closely resembles a Santa Clara ranch that London had once visited. When Buck is stolen by a man whose gambling weakness is akin to London's mother's, he is put on the train at College Park, a depot between Santa Clara and San Jose that London knew well. Later Buck travels through the "great railway depot" in Oakland, which was close to one of London's boyhood homes. And on a less literal level, as Buck struggled first to adapt to a new environment and then to master it, so London endeavored to establish himself in the literary world that was so alien to him and his family.

Other readers have seen how the tale fits within the traditions of literary realism and naturalism that were flourishing at the time. Buck is a Darwinian dog, surviving because he is fit, because he is adaptable, because he is inexorable, knowing and adhering strictly to the law of "kill or be killed, eat or be eaten," and because—after all—he has the quality that makes for greatness—imagination.

Still other readers have pointed out the timeless mythological aspects of Buck's story. Like the heroes who populate the world's great myths, Buck hears the call to adventure, undergoes a period of education, experiences a kind of death, returns to life even greater than before, receives a precious gift (the love of John Thornton), and eventually achieves his apotheosis as the Ghost Dog of Yeehat Indian legend.

The Call of the Wild would never have enjoyed its century of acclaim, however, if it had been a simple dog story, if it had been a thinly disguised autobiography of Jack London, a Darwinian parable, or even a poetic myth with ancient rhythms and themes. No, the novel has endured because, like all great literature, it grips the reader's imagination and mind even as it informs the heart.

Chronology of Events in The Call of the Wild

"AND THIS IS the manner of dog Buck was in the fall of 1897," wrote London, "when the Klondike strike dragged men from all the world into the frozen North." This date—which appears in the sixth paragraph of the novel—is the only one in the entire text. London does, however, occasionally mention intervals of time. Days pass, he tells us. Weeks. Months. Seasons. Using these few references and working with published records of freeze-up and breakup dates on the Yukon River, I have been able to establish a rough chronology of events in the novel. The specific dates I have listed are approximate and arbitrary—after all, London was writing a piece of fiction, not a travelogue; however, the estimated dates are consistent with one another. (From his notes and manuscripts stored at the Huntington Library, in San Marino, California, we know that London prepared just such a rough chronology for his *White Fang;* however, very little material remains from the period when London was working on *The Call of the Wild.*)

30 October 1897: Manuel steals Buck and puts him on a Southern Pacific train at College Park (midway between San Jose and Santa Clara), about three miles from Judge Miller's ranch. Buck rides in a baggage car to San Francisco (about fifty miles north), a trip of about an hour and a half to two hours. Buck spends the night in a shed in the back of a waterfront saloon—about two miles from the Southern Pacific depot in San Francisco.

31 October 1897: Buck rides a Southern Pacific ferry across San Francisco Bay to Oakland, where he boards a Southern Pacific train to Seattle (changing to Northern Pacific in Portland, Oregon).

2 November 1897: After a journey of two days and two nights Buck arrives in Seattle, where he joins other dogs at a place operated by "the man in the red sweater." We don't know how long Buck is in Seattle ("days went by," London tells us), but he is eventually purchased for $300 by Perrault, a courier for the Canadian government.

16 November 1897: Buck leaves Seattle aboard the *Narwhal* for Dyea, Alaska, a journey requiring four to seven days.

21 November 1897: Buck arrives in Dyea; sees Curly killed in front of the log store; and undergoes some rudimentary training with a sled.

22 November 1897: Buck leaves Dyea on the Chilkoot Trail for Dawson City. We know that the team is the first one on the ice that winter and that one portion of the river (the Thirtymile) is not completely frozen. In 1897 the river closed at Dawson on 13 November; it would have frozen about two weeks later at Whitehorse.

1 December 1897: On the shore of Lake Laberge, about eighty starving huskies attack the team at their campsite.

22 December 1897: The team arrives at Dawson City, Yukon, at the confluence of the Yukon and Klondike rivers.

29 December 1897: After a week's rest, the team leaves Dawson City.

5 January 1898: Buck kills Spitz at the mouth of the Takhini River. (This is an error in geography; see annotation on page 92.)

11 January 1898: The team arrives in Skagway—a record run of fourteen days.

15 January 1898: A "Scotch half-breed"—a mail carrier for the Canadian government—takes over the team; they leave for Dawson once again. Along the way, Buck begins having his visions of the prehistoric man.

12 February 1898: The team arrives in Dawson.

15 February 1898: The team leaves Dawson.

10 March 1898: Dave is shot a day's journey away from Cassiar Bar.

17 March 1898: The team—"in a wretched state, worn out and worn down"—arrives in Skagway.

21 March 1898: Hal and Charles purchase the team.

22 March 1898: The team leaves once again for Dawson City.

6 May 1898: At the mouth of the White River, about eighty miles short of Dawson City, Hal, Charles, Mercedes, and the few remaining dogs fall through the ice and die. (In 1898 ice on the Yukon River broke at Dawson City on 8 May.) John Thornton rescues Buck.

1 June 1898: Buck—now fully recovered—goes with Thornton, Hans, Pete, and their dogs (Skeet and Nig) as they float a raft of sawlogs downriver to Dawson.

15 June 1898: Thornton commands Buck to jump from a cliff near the headwaters of the Tanana River in Alaska.

15 July 1898: Buck attacks "Black" Burton after he punches John Thornton in a bar in Circle City, Alaska.

1 September 1898: Buck rescues John Thornton in the rapids of the Fortymile River, Yukon Territory.

2 January 1899: Buck wins the sled-pulling wager outside the Eldorado Saloon in Dawson City.

9 January 1899: Thornton and his partners leave with Buck and the other dogs to search for the legendary Lost Cabin mine, hundreds of miles east of Dawson City in the Mackenzie Mountains.

21 June 1899: The search continues—amid "summer blizzards" and under the midnight sun.

1 September 1899: They enter a "weird lake country" where nothing appears to be alive.

June 1900: "Spring came on once more," and Thornton and his partners find a rich gold deposit.

15 July 1900: Buck runs with the timber wolf—his "wild brother."

16 July 1900: Buck returns to camp at dinner time.

17–18 July 1900: Buck stays in camp, close to Thornton.

19–31 July 1900: Away from camp for "days at a time," Buck wanders "for a week," during which time he kills a black bear and two wolverines, scattering the others "like chaff."

1 September 1900: Moose appear in the territory.

2–5 September 1900: Buck stalks and kills a bull moose wounded by an arrow.

6 September 1900: Buck remains by his kill, feeding.

7 September 1900: Yeehats attack, killing all men and dogs in Thornton's camp. Buck kills some of the Yeehats, then broods all day by the pool that holds Thornton's body. Wolves arrive that night; Buck battles them, is accepted by the pack, and runs off with them.

July 1903: "The years were not many" when the Yeehats began to notice a change in the breed of timber wolves. (The Macmillan Company publishes *The Call of the Wild* by Jack London.)

The Call
of the Wild

ANNOTATED AND ILLUSTRATED

CHAPTER ONE

Into the Primitive

"Old longings nomadic leap,
Chafing at custom's chain;
Again from its brumal sleep
Wakens the ferine strain."

1 BUCK DID NOT read the newspapers, or he would have known that trouble was brewing, not alone for himself, but for every tide-water dog, strong of muscle and with warm, long hair, from Puget Sound to San Diego. Because men, groping in the Arctic darkness, had found a yellow metal, and because steamship and transportation companies 5 were booming the find, thousands of men were rushing into the Northland. These men wanted dogs, and the dogs they wanted were heavy dogs, with strong muscles by which to toil, and furry coats to protect them from the frost.

Buck lived at a big house in the sun-kissed Santa Clara Valley. Judge Miller's place, it was called. It stood back from the road, half hidden among the trees, through 10 which glimpses could be caught of the wide cool veranda that ran around its four sides. The house was approached by gravelled driveways which wound about through wide-spreading lawns and under the interlacing boughs of tall poplars. At the rear things were on even a more spacious scale than at the front. There were great stables, where a dozen grooms and boys held forth, rows of vine-clad servants' cottages, an endless and 15 orderly array of outhouses, long grape arbors, green pastures, orchards, and berry patches. Then there was the pumping plant for the artesian well, and the big cement tank where Judge Miller's boys took their morning plunge and kept cool in the hot afternoon.

And over this great demesne Buck ruled. Here he was born, and here he had lived the four years of his life. It was true, there were other dogs. There could not but be other dogs on so vast a place, but they did not count. They came and went, resided in the populous kennels, or lived obscurely in the recesses of the house after the fashion of Toots, the Japanese pug, or Ysabel, the Mexican hairless,—strange creatures that rarely put nose out of doors or set foot to ground. On the other hand, there were the fox terriers, a score of them at least, who yelped fearful promises at Toots and Ysabel looking out of the windows at them and protected by a legion of housemaids armed with brooms and mops.

But Buck was neither house-dog nor kennel-dog. The whole realm was his. He plunged into the swimming tank or went hunting with the Judge's sons; he escorted Mollie and Alice, the Judge's daughters, on long twilight or early morning rambles; on wintry nights he lay at the Judge's feet before the roaring library fire; he carried the Judge's grandsons on his back, or rolled them in the grass, and guarded their footsteps through wild adventures down to the fountain in the stable yard, and even beyond, where the paddocks were, and the berry patches. Among the terriers he stalked imperiously, and Toots and Ysabel he utterly ignored, for he was king,—king over all creeping, crawling, flying things of Judge Miller's place, humans included.

His father, Elmo, a huge St. Bernard, had been the Judge's inseparable companion, and Buck bid fair to follow in the way of his father. He was not so large,—he weighed only one hundred and forty pounds,—for his mother, Shep, had been a Scotch shepherd dog. Nevertheless, one hundred and forty pounds, to which was added the dignity that comes of good living and universal respect, enabled him to carry himself in right royal fashion. During the four years since his puppyhood he had lived the life of a sated aristocrat; he had a fine pride in himself, was even a trifle egotistical, as country gentlemen sometimes become because of their insular situation. But he had saved himself by not becoming a mere pampered house-dog. Hunting and kindred outdoor delights had kept down the fat and hardened his muscles; and to him, as to the cold-tubbing races, the love of water had been a tonic and a health preserver.

And this was the manner of dog Buck was in the fall of 1897, when the Klondike strike dragged men from all the world into the frozen North. But Buck did not read the newspapers, and he did not know that Manuel, one of the gardener's helpers, was an undesirable acquaintance. Manuel had one besetting sin. He loved to play Chinese lottery. Also, in his gambling, he had one besetting weakness—faith in a system; and this made his damnation certain. For to play a system requires money, while the wages of a gardener's helper do not lap over the needs of a wife and numerous progeny.

The Judge was at a meeting of the Raisin Growers' Association, and the boys were busy organizing an athletic club, on the memorable night of Manuel's treachery. No one saw him and Buck go off through the orchard on what Buck imagined was merely a stroll. And with the exception of a solitary man, no one saw them arrive at the little flag station known as College Park. This man talked with Manuel, and money chinked between them.

"You might wrap up the goods before you deliver 'm," the stranger said gruffly, and Manuel doubled a piece of stout rope around Buck's neck under the collar.

"Twist it, an' you'll choke 'm plentee," said Manuel, and the stranger grunted a ready affirmative.

Buck had accepted the rope with quiet dignity. To be sure, it was an unwonted performance: but he had learned to trust in men he knew, and to give them credit for a wisdom that outreached his own. But when the ends of the rope were placed in the stranger's hands, he growled menacingly. He had merely intimated his displeasure, in his pride believing that to intimate was to command. But to his surprise the rope tightened around his neck, shutting off his breath. In quick rage he sprang at the man, who met him halfway, grappled him close by the throat, and with a deft twist threw him over on his back. Then the rope tightened mercilessly, while Buck struggled in a fury, his tongue lolling out of his mouth and his great chest panting futilely. Never in all his life had he been so vilely treated, and never in all his life had he been so angry. But his strength ebbed, his eyes glazed, and he knew nothing when the train was flagged and the two men threw him into the baggage car.

The next he knew, he was dimly aware that his tongue was hurting and that he was being jolted along in some kind of a conveyance. The hoarse shriek of a locomotive whistling a crossing told him where he was. He had travelled too often with the Judge not to know the sensation of riding in a baggage car. He opened his eyes, and into them came the unbridled anger of a kidnapped king. The man sprang for his throat, but Buck was too quick for him. His jaws closed on the hand, nor did they relax till his senses were choked out of him once more.

"Yep, has fits," the man said, hiding his mangled hand from the baggageman, who had been attracted by the sounds of struggle. "I'm takin' 'm up for the boss to 'Frisco. A crack dog-doctor there thinks that he can cure 'm."

Concerning that night's ride, the man spoke most eloquently for himself, in a little shed back of a saloon on the San Francisco water front.

"All I get is fifty for it," he grumbled; "an' I wouldn't do it over for a thousand, cold cash."

His hand was wrapped in a bloody handkerchief, and the right trouser leg was ripped from knee to ankle.

"How much did the other mug get?" the saloon-keeper demanded.

"A hundred," was the reply. "Wouldn't take a sou less, so help me."

"That makes a hundred and fifty," the saloon-keeper calculated; "and he's worth it, or I'm a squarehead."

The kidnapper undid the bloody wrappings and looked at his lacerated hand. "If I don't get the hydrophoby—"

"It'll be because you was born to hang," laughed the saloon-keeper. "Here, lend me a hand before you pull your freight," he added.

Dazed, suffering intolerable pain from throat and tongue, with the life half throttled out of him, Buck attempted to face his tormentors. But he was thrown down and choked repeatedly, till they succeeded in filing the heavy brass collar from off his neck. Then the rope was removed, and he was flung into a cagelike crate.

There he lay for the remainder of the weary night, nursing his wrath and wounded pride. He could not understand what it all meant. What did they want with him, these strange men? Why were they keeping him pent up in this narrow crate? He did not know why, but he felt oppressed by the vague sense of impending calamity. Several times during the night he sprang to his feet when the shed door rattled open, expecting to see the Judge, or the boys at least. But each time it was the bulging face of the saloon-keeper that peered in at him by the sickly light of a tallow candle. And each time the joyful bark that trembled in Buck's throat was twisted into a savage growl.

But the saloon-keeper let him alone, and in the morning four men entered and picked up the crate. More tormentors, Buck decided, for they were evil-looking creatures, ragged and unkempt; and he stormed and raged at them through the bars. They only laughed and poked sticks at him, which he promptly assailed with this teeth till he realized that that was what they wanted. Whereupon he lay down sullenly and allowed the crate to be lifted into a wagon. Then he, and the crate in which he was imprisoned, began a passage through many hands. Clerks in the express office took charge of him; he was carted about in another wagon; a truck carried him, with an assortment of boxes and parcels, upon a ferry steamer; he was trucked off the steamer into a great railway depot, and finally he was deposited in an express car.

For two days and nights this express car was dragged along at the tail of shrieking locomotives; and for two days and nights Buck neither ate nor drank. In his anger he had met the first advances of the express messengers with growls, and they had retaliated by teasing him. When he flung himself against the bars, quivering and frothing, they laughed at him and taunted him. They growled and barked like detestable dogs, mewed, and flapped their arms and crowed. It was all very silly, he knew; but therefore the more outrage to his dignity, and his anger waxed and waxed. He did not mind the hunger so much, but the lack of water caused him severe suffering and fanned his wrath to fever-pitch. For that matter, high-strung and finely sensitive, the ill treatment had flung him into a fever, which was fed by the inflammation of his parched and swollen throat and tongue.

He was glad for one thing: the rope was off his neck. That had given them an unfair advantage; but now that it was off, he would show them. They would never get another rope around his neck. Upon that he was resolved. For two days and nights he neither ate nor drank, and during those two days and nights of torment, he accumulated a fund of wrath that boded ill for whoever first fell foul of him. His eyes turned bloodshot, and he was metamorphosed into a raging fiend. So changed was he that the Judge himself would not have recognized him; and the express messengers breathed with relief when they bundled him off the train at Seattle.

Four men gingerly carried the crate from the wagon into a small, high-walled back yard. A stout man, with a red sweater that sagged generously at the neck, came out and signed the book for the driver. That was the man, Buck divined, the next tormentor, and he hurled himself savagely against the bars. The man smiled grimly, and brought a hatchet and a club.

"You ain't going to take him out now?" the driver asked.

"Sure," the man replied, driving the hatchet into the crate for a pry.

There was an instantaneous scattering of the four men who had carried it in, and from safe perches on top the wall they prepared to watch the performance.

Buck rushed at the splintering wood, sinking his teeth into it, surging and wrestling with it. Wherever the hatchet fell on the outside, he was there on the inside, snarling and growling, as furiously anxious to get out as the man in the red sweater was calmly intent on getting him out.

155   "Now, you red-eyed devil," he said, when he had made an opening sufficient for the passage of Buck's body. At the same time he dropped the hatchet and shifted the club to his right hand.

   And Buck was truly a red-eyed devil, as he drew himself together for the spring, hair bristling, mouth foaming, a mad glitter in his blood-shot eyes. Straight at the man

160 he launched his one hundred and forty pounds of fury, surcharged with the pent passion of two days and nights. In mid air, just as his jaws were about to close on the man, he received a shock that checked his body and brought his teeth together with an agonizing clip. He whirled over, fetching the ground on his back and side. He had never been struck by a club in his life, and did not understand. With a snarl that was part bark and

165 more scream he was again on his feet and launched into the air. And again the shock came and he was brought crushingly to the ground. This time he was aware that it was the club, but his madness knew no caution. A dozen times he charged, and as often the club broke the charge and smashed him down.

   After a particularly fierce blow, he crawled to his feet, too dazed to rush. He

170 staggered limply about, the blood flowing from nose and mouth and ears, his beautiful coat sprayed and flecked with bloody slaver. Then the man advanced and deliberately dealt him a frightful blow on the nose. All the pain he had endured was as nothing compared with the exquisite agony of this. With a roar that was almost lionlike in its ferocity, he again hurled himself at the man. But the man, shifting the club from right to

175 left, coolly caught him by the under jaw, at the same time wrenching downward and backward. Buck described a complete circle in the air, and half of another, then crashed to the ground on his head and chest.

   For the last time he rushed. The man struck the shrewd blow he had purposely withheld for so long, and Buck crumpled up and went down, knocked utterly senseless.

180   "He's no slouch at dog-breakin', that's wot I say," one of the men on the wall cried enthusiastically.

   "Druther break cayuses any day, and twice on Sundays," was the reply of the driver, as he climbed on the wagon and started the horses.

   Buck's senses came back to him, but not his strength. He lay where he had fallen,

185 and from there he watched the man in the red sweater.

   "'Answers to the name of Buck,'" the man soliloquized, quoting from the saloon-keeper's letter which had announced the consignment of the crate and contents. "Well, Buck, my boy," he went on in a genial voice, "we've had our little ruction, and the best thing we can do is to let it go at that. You've learned your place, and I know mine.

190 Be a good dog and all 'll go well and the goose hang high. Be a bad dog, and I'll whale the stuffin' outa you. Understand?"

As he spoke he fearlessly patted the head he had so mercilessly pounded, and though Buck's hair involuntarily bristled at touch of the hand, he endured it without protest. When the man brought him water he drank eagerly, and later bolted a generous
195 meal of raw meat, chunk by chunk, from the man's hand.

He was beaten (he knew that); but he was not broken. He saw, once for all, that he stood no chance against a man with a club. He had learned the lesson, and in all his after life he never forgot it. That club was a revelation. It was his introduction to the reign of primitive law, and he met the introduction half-way. The facts of life took on a
200 fiercer aspect; and while he faced that aspect uncowed, he faced it with all the latent cunning of his nature aroused. As the days went by, other dogs came, in crates and at the ends of ropes, some docilely, and some raging and roaring as he had come; and, one and all, he watched them pass under the dominion of the man in the red sweater. Again and again, as he looked at each brutal performance, the lesson was driven home to Buck:
205 a man with a club was a lawgiver, a master to be obeyed, though not necessarily conciliated. Of this last Buck was never guilty, though he did see beaten dogs that fawned upon the man, and wagged their tails, and licked his hand. Also he saw one dog, that would neither conciliate nor obey, finally killed in the struggle for mastery.

Now and again men came, strangers, who talked excitedly, wheedlingly, and in all
210 kinds of fashions to the man in the red sweater. And at such times that money passed between them the strangers took one or more of the dogs away with them. Buck wondered where they went, for they never came back; but the fear of the future was strong upon him, and he was glad each time when he was not selected.

Yet his time came, in the end, in the form of a little weazened man who spat
215 broken English and many strange and uncouth exclamations which Buck could not understand.

"Sacredam!" he cried, when his eyes lit upon Buck. "Dat one dam bully dog? Eh? How moch?"

"Three hundred, and a present at that," was the prompt reply of the man in the
220 red sweater. "And seein' it's government money, you ain't got no kick coming, eh, Perrault?"

Perrault grinned. Considering that the price of dogs had been boomed skyward by the unwonted demand, it was not an unfair sum for so fine an animal. The Canadian Government would be no loser, nor would its despatches travel the slower. Perrault

225   knew dogs, and when he looked at Buck he knew that he was one in a thousand— "One in ten t'ousand," he commented mentally.

    Buck saw money pass between them, and was not surprised when Curly, a good-natured Newfoundland, and he were led away by the little weazened man. That was the last he saw of the man in the red sweater, and as Curly and he looked at

230   receding Seattle from the deck of the *Narwhal,* it was the last he saw of the warm Southland. Curly and he were taken below by Perrault and turned over to a black-faced giant called François. Perrault was a French-Canadian, and swarthy; but François was a French-Canadian half-breed, and twice as swarthy. They were a new kind of men to Buck (of which he was destined to see many more), and while he developed no affection

235   for them, he none the less grew honestly to respect them. He speedily learned that Perrault and François were fair men, calm and impartial in administering justice, and too wise in the way of dogs to be fooled by dogs.

    In the 'tween-decks of the *Narwhal,* Buck and Curly joined two other dogs. One of them was a big, snow-white fellow from Spitzbergen who had been brought away by a

240   whaling captain, and who had later accompanied a Geological Survey into the Barrens. He was friendly, in a treacherous sort of way, smiling into one's face the while he meditated some underhand trick, as, for instance, when he stole from Buck's food at the first meal. As Buck sprang to punish him, the lash of François's whip sang through the air, reaching the culprit first; and nothing remained to Buck but to recover the bone.

245   That was fair of François, he decided, and the half-breed began his rise in Buck's estimation.

    The other dog made no advances, nor received any; also, he did not attempt to steal from the newcomers. He was a gloomy, morose fellow, and he showed Curly plainly that all he desired was to be left alone, and further, that there would be trouble if

250   he were not left alone. "Dave" he was called, and he ate and slept, or yawned between times, and took interest in nothing, not even when the *Narwhal* crossed Queen Charlotte Sound and rolled and pitched and bucked like a thing possessed. When Buck and Curly grew excited, half wild with fear, he raised his head as though annoyed, favored them with an incurious glance, yawned, and went to sleep again.

255   Day and night the ship throbbed to the tireless pulse of the propeller, and though one day was very like another, it was apparent to Buck that the weather was steadily growing colder. At last, one morning, the propeller was quiet, and the *Narwhal* was pervaded with an atmosphere of excitement. He felt it, as did the other dogs, and knew that a change was at hand. François leashed them and brought them on deck. At the

260   first step upon the cold surface, Buck's feet sank into a white mushy something very like mud. He sprang back with a snort. More of this white stuff was falling through the air. He shook himself, but more of it fell upon him. He sniffed it curiously, then licked some up on his tongue. It bit like fire, and the next instant was gone. This puzzled him. He tried it again, with the same result. The onlookers laughed uproariously, and he felt

265   ashamed, he knew not why, for it was his first snow.

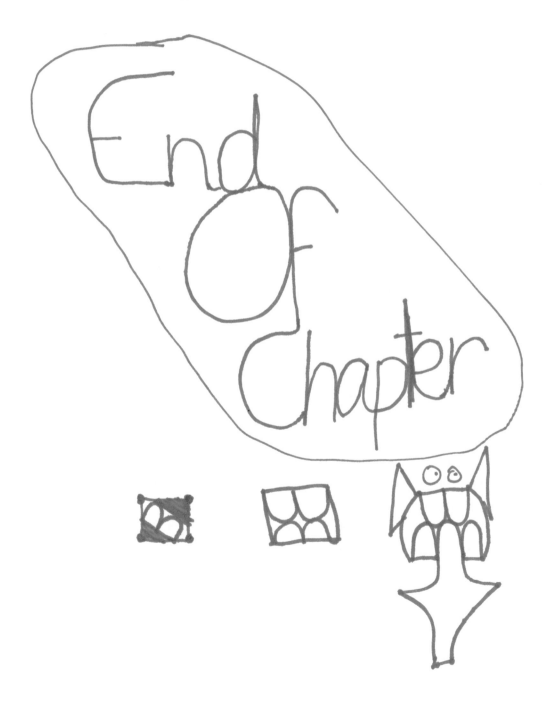

CHAPTER TWO

The Law of Club and Fang

BUCK'S FIRST DAY on the Dyea beach was like a nightmare. Every hour was filled with shock and surprise. He had been suddenly jerked from the heart of civilization and flung into the heart of things primordial. No lazy, sun-kissed life was this, with nothing to do but loaf and be bored. Here was neither peace, nor rest, nor a moment's safety. All
270 was confusion and action, and every moment life and limb were in peril. There was imperative need to be constantly alert; for these dogs and men were not town dogs and men. They were savages, all of them, who knew no law but the law of club and fang.

He had never seen dogs fight as these wolfish creatures fought, and his first experience taught him an unforgetable lesson. It is true, it was a vicarious experience,
275 else he would not have lived to profit by it. Curly was the victim. They were camped near the log store, where she, in her friendly way, made advances to a husky dog the size of a full-grown wolf, though not half so large as she. There was no warning, only a leap in like a flash, a metallic clip of teeth, a leap out equally swift, and Curly's face was ripped open from eye to jaw.

280 It was the wolf manner of fighting, to strike and leap away; but there was more to it than this. Thirty or forty huskies ran to the spot and surrounded the combatants in an intent and silent circle. Buck did not comprehend that silent intentness, nor the eager way with which they were licking their chops. Curly rushed her antagonist, who struck again and leaped aside. He met her next rush with his chest, in a peculiar fashion that

12

285 tumbled her off her feet. She never regained them. This was what the onlooking huskies had waited for. They closed in upon her, snarling and yelping, and she was buried, screaming with agony, beneath the bristling mass of bodies.

So sudden was it, and so unexpected, that Buck was taken aback. He saw Spitz run out his scarlet tongue in a way he had of laughing; and he saw François, swinging an
290 axe, spring into the mess of dogs. Three men with clubs were helping him to scatter them. It did not take long. Two minutes from the time Curly went down, the last of her assailants were clubbed off. But she lay there limp and lifeless in the bloody, trampled snow, almost literally torn to pieces, the swart half-breed standing over her and cursing horribly. The scene often came back to Buck to trouble him in his sleep. So that was
295 the way. No fair play. Once down, that was the end of you. Well, he would see to it that he never went down. Spitz ran out his tongue and laughed again, and from that moment Buck hated him with a bitter and deathless hatred.

Before he had recovered from the shock caused by the tragic passing of Curly, he received another shock. François fastened upon him an arrangement of straps and
300 buckles. It was a harness, such as he had seen the grooms put on the horses at home. And as he had seen horses work, so he was set to work, hauling François on a sled to the forest that fringed the valley, and returning with a load of firewood. Though his dignity was sorely hurt by thus being made a draught animal, he was too wise to rebel. He buckled down with a will and did his best, though it was all new and strange. François
305 was stern, demanding instant obedience, and by virtue of his whip receiving instant obedience; while Dave, who was an experienced wheeler, nipped Buck's hind quarters whenever he was in error. Spitz was the leader, likewise experienced, and while he could not always get at Buck, he growled sharp reproof now and again, or cunningly threw his weight in the traces to jerk Buck into the way he should go. Buck learned easily, and
310 under the combined tuition of his two mates and François made remarkable progress. Ere they returned to camp he knew enough to stop at "ho," to go ahead at "mush," to swing wide on the bends, and to keep clear of the wheeler when the loaded sled shot downhill at their heels.

"T'ree vair' good dogs," François told Perrault. "Dat Buck, heem pool lak hell. I
315 tich heem queek as anyt'ing."

By afternoon, Perrault, who was in a hurry to be on the trail with his despatches, returned with two more dogs. "Billee" and "Joe" he called them, two brothers, and true huskies both. Sons of the one mother though they were, they were as different as day and night. Billee's one fault was his excessive good nature, while Joe was the very

320 opposite, sour and introspective, with a perpetual snarl and a malignant eye. Buck received them in comradely fashion, Dave ignored them, while Spitz proceeded to thrash first one and then the other. Billee wagged his tail appeasingly, turned to run when he saw that appeasement was of no avail, and cried (still appeasingly) when Spitz's sharp teeth scored his flank. But no matter how Spitz circled, Joe whirled around on his heels

325 to face him, mane bristling, ears laid back, lips writhing and snarling, jaws clipping together as fast as he could snap, and eyes diabolically gleaming—the incarnation of belligerent fear. So terrible was his appearance that Spitz was forced to forego disciplining him; but to cover his own discomfiture he turned upon the inoffensive and wailing Billee and drove him to the confines of the camp.

330 By evening Perrault secured another dog, an old husky, long and lean and gaunt, with a battle-scarred face and a single eye which flashed a warning of prowess that commanded respect. He was called Sol-leks, which means the Angry One. Like Dave, he asked nothing, gave nothing, expected nothing; and when he marched slowly and deliberately into their midst, even Spitz left him alone. He had one peculiarity which

335 Buck was unlucky enough to discover. He did not like to be approached on his blind side. Of this offence Buck was unwittingly guilty, and the first knowledge he had of his indiscretion was when Sol-leks whirled upon him and slashed his shoulder to the bone for three inches up and down. Forever after Buck avoided his blind side, and to the last of their comradeship had no more trouble. His only apparent ambition, like Dave's, was to

340 be left alone; though, as Buck was afterward to learn, each of them possessed one other and even more vital ambition.

That night Buck faced the great problem of sleeping. The tent, illumined by a candle, glowed warmly in the midst of the white plain; and when he, as a matter of course, entered it, both Perrault and François bombarded him with curses and cooking

345 utensils, till he recovered from his consternation and fled ignominiously into the outer cold. A chill wind was blowing that nipped him sharply and bit with especial venom into his wounded shoulder. He lay down on the snow and attempted to sleep, but the frost soon drove him shivering to his feet. Miserable and disconsolate, he wandered about among the many tents, only to find that one place was as cold as another. Here and

350 there savage dogs rushed upon him, but he bristled his neck-hair and snarled (for he was learning fast), and they let him go his way unmolested.

Finally an idea came to him. He would return and see how his own team-mates were making out. To his astonishment, they had disappeared. Again he wandered about through the great camp, looking for them, and again he returned. Were they in the tent?

355 No, that could not be, else he would not have been driven out. Then where could they possibly be? With drooping tail and shivering body, very forlorn indeed, he aimlessly circled the tent. Suddenly the snow gave way beneath his fore legs and he sank down. Something wriggled under his feet. He sprang back, bristling and snarling, fearful of the unseen and unknown. But a friendly little yelp reassured him, and he went back to
360 investigate. A whiff of warm air ascended to his nostrils, and there, curled up under the snow in a snug ball, lay Billee. He whined placatingly, squirmed and wriggled to show his good will and intentions, and even ventured, as a bribe for peace, to lick Buck's face with his warm wet tongue.

Another lesson. So that was the way they did it, eh? Buck confidently selected a
365 spot, and with much fuss and waste effort proceeded to dig a hole for himself. In a trice the heat from his body filled the confined space and he was asleep. The day had been long and arduous, and he slept soundly and comfortably, though he growled and barked and wrestled with bad dreams.

Nor did he open his eyes till roused by the noises of the waking camp. At first he
370 did not know where he was. It had snowed during the night and he was completely buried. The snow walls pressed him on every side, and a great surge of fear swept through him—the fear of the wild thing for the trap. It was a token that he was harking back through his own life to the lives of his forebears; for he was a civilized dog, an unduly civilized dog, and of his own experience knew no trap and so could not of himself
375 fear it. The muscles of his whole body contracted spasmodically and instinctively, the hair on his neck and shoulders stood on end, and with a ferocious snarl he bounded straight up into the blinding day, the snow flying about him in a flashing cloud. Ere he landed on his feet, he saw the white camp spread out before him and knew where he was and remembered all that had passed from the time he went for a stroll with Manuel to
380 the hole he had dug for himself the night before.

A shout from François hailed his appearance. "Wot I say?" the dog-driver cried to Perrault. "Dat Buck for sure learn queek as anyt'ing."

Perrault nodded gravely. As courier for the Canadian Government, bearing important despatches, he was anxious to secure the best dogs, and he was particularly
385 gladdened by the possession of Buck.

Three more huskies were added to the team inside an hour, making a total of nine, and before another quarter of an hour had passed they were in harness and swinging up the trail toward the Dyea Cañon. Buck was glad to be gone, and though the work was hard he found he did not particularly despise it. He was surprised at the

390 eagerness which animated the whole team and which was communicated to him; but still more surprising was the change wrought in Dave and Sol-leks. They were new dogs, utterly transformed by the harness. All passiveness and unconcern had dropped from them. They were alert and active, anxious that the work should go well, and fiercely irritable with whatever, by delay or confusion, retarded that work. The toil of the traces 395 seemed the supreme expression of their being, and all that they lived for and the only thing in which they took delight.

Dave was wheeler or sled dog, pulling in front of him was Buck, then came Sol-leks; the rest of the team was strung out ahead, single file, to the leader, which position was filled by Spitz.

400 Buck had been purposely placed between Dave and Sol-leks so that he might receive instruction. Apt scholar that he was, they were equally apt teachers, never allowing him to linger long in error, and enforcing their teaching with their sharp teeth. Dave was fair and very wise. He never nipped Buck without cause, and he never failed to nip him when he stood in need of it. As François's whip backed him up, Buck found 405 it to be cheaper to mend his ways than to retaliate. Once, during a brief halt, when he got tangled in the traces and delayed the start, both Dave and Sol-leks flew at him and administered a sound trouncing. The resulting tangle was even worse, but Buck took good care to keep the traces clear thereafter; and ere the day was done, so well had he mastered his work, his mates about ceased nagging him. François's whip snapped less 410 frequently, and Perrault even honored Buck by lifting up his feet and carefully examining them.

It was a hard day's run, up the Cañon, through Sheep Camp, past the Scales and the timber line, across glaciers and snowdrifts hundreds of feet deep, and over the great Chilcoot Divide, which stands between the salt water and the fresh and guards 415 forbiddingly the sad and lonely North. They made good time down the chain of lakes which fills the craters of extinct volcanoes, and late that night pulled into the huge camp at the head of Lake Bennett, where thousands of gold-seekers were building boats against the break-up of the ice in the spring. Buck made his hole in the snow and slept the sleep of the exhausted just, but all too early was routed out in the cold darkness and 420 harnessed with his mates to the sled.

That day they made forty miles, the trail being packed; but the next day, and for many days to follow, they broke their own trail, worked harder, and made poorer time. As a rule, Perrault travelled ahead of the team, packing the snow with webbed shoes to make it easier for them. François, guiding the sled at the gee-pole, sometimes exchanged

425 places with him, but not often. Perrault was in a hurry, and he prided himself on his knowledge of ice, which knowledge was indispensable, for the fall ice was very thin, and where there was swift water, there was no ice at all.

Day after day, for days unending, Buck toiled in the traces. Always, they broke camp in the dark, and the first gray of dawn found them hitting the trail with fresh miles 430 reeled off behind them. And always they pitched camp after dark, eating their bit of fish, and crawling to sleep into the snow. Buck was ravenous. The pound and half of sun-dried salmon, which was his ration for each day, seemed to go nowhere. He never had enough, and suffered from perpetual hunger pangs. Yet the other dogs, because they weighed less and were born to the life, received a pound only of the fish and 435 managed to keep in good condition.

He swiftly lost the fastidiousness which had characterized his old life. A dainty eater, he found that his mates, finishing first, robbed him of his unfinished ration. There was no defending it. While he was fighting off two or three, it was disappearing down the throats of the others. To remedy this, he ate as fast as they; and, so greatly did 440 hunger compel him, he was not above taking what did not belong to him. He watched and learned. When he saw Pike, one of the new dogs, a clever malingerer and thief, slyly steal a slice of bacon when Perrault's back was turned, he duplicated the performance the following day, getting away with the whole chunk. A great uproar was raised, but he was unsuspected; while Dub, an awkward blunderer who was always getting caught, was 445 punished for Buck's misdeed.

This first theft marked Buck as fit to survive in the hostile Northland environment. It marked his adaptability, his capacity to adjust himself to changing conditions, the lack of which would have meant swift and terrible death. It marked, further, the decay or going to pieces of his moral nature, a vain thing and a handicap in the ruthless struggle 450 for existence. It was all well enough in the Southland, under the law of love and fellowship, to respect private property and personal feelings; but in the Northland, under the law of club and fang, whoso took such things into account was a fool, and in so far as he observed them he would fail to prosper.

Not that Buck reasoned it out. He was fit, that was all, and unconsciously he 455 accommodated himself to the new mode of life. All his days, no matter what the odds, he had never run from a fight. But the club of the man in the red sweater had beaten into him a more fundamental and primitive code. Civilized, he could have died for a moral consideration, say the defence of Judge Miller's riding-whip; but the completeness of his decivilization was now evidenced by his ability to flee from the defence of a moral

460 consideration and so save his hide. He did not steal for joy of it, but because of the clamor of his stomach. He did not rob openly, but stole secretly and cunningly, out of respect for club and fang. In short, the things he did were done because it was easier to do them than not to do them.

His development (or retrogression) was rapid. His muscles became hard as iron, 465 and he grew callous to all ordinary pain. He achieved an internal as well as external economy. He could eat anything, no matter how loathsome or indigestible; and, once eaten, the juices of his stomach extracted the last least particle of nutriment; and his blood carried it to the farthest reaches of his body, building it into the toughest and stoutest of tissues. Sight and scent became remarkably keen, while his hearing developed 470 such acuteness that in his sleep he heard the faintest sound and knew whether it heralded peace or peril. He learned to bite the ice out with his teeth when it collected between his toes; and when he was thirsty and there was a thick scum of ice over the water hole, he would break it by rearing and striking it with stiff fore legs. His most conspicuous trait was an ability to scent the wind and forecast it a night in advance. No 475 matter how breathless the air when he dug his nest by tree or bank, the wind that later blew inevitably found him to leeward, sheltered and snug.

And not only did he learn by experience, but instincts long dead became alive again. The domesticated generations fell from him. In vague ways he remembered back to the youth of the breed, to the time the wild dogs ranged in packs through the primeval 480 forest and killed their meat as they ran it down. It was no task for him to learn to fight with cut and slash and the quick wolf snap. In this manner had fought forgotten ancestors. They quickened the old life within him, and the old tricks which they had stamped into the heredity of the breed were his tricks. They came to him without effort or discovery, as though they had been his always. And when, on the still cold nights, he 485 pointed his nose at a star and howled long and wolflike, it was his ancestors, dead and dust, pointing nose at star and howling down through the centuries and through him. And his cadences were their cadences, the cadences which voiced their woe and what to them was the meaning of the stillness, and the cold, and dark.

Thus, as token of what a puppet thing life is, the ancient song surged through him 490 and he came into his own again; and he came because men had found a yellow metal in the North, and because Manuel was a gardener's helper whose wages did not lap over the needs of his wife and divers small copies of himself.

CHAPTER THREE

The Dominant Primordial Beast

THE DOMINANT PRIMORDIAL beast was strong in Buck, and under the fierce conditions of trail life it grew and grew. Yet it was a secret growth. His new-born cunning gave him poise and control. He was too busy adjusting himself to the new life to feel at ease, and not only did he not pick fights, but he avoided them whenever possible. A certain deliberateness characterized his attitude. He was not prone to rashness and precipitate action; and in the bitter hatred between him and Spitz he betrayed no impatience, shunned all offensive acts.

On the other hand, possibly because he divined in Buck a dangerous rival, Spitz never lost an opportunity of showing his teeth. He even went out of his way to bully Buck, striving constantly to start the fight which could end only in the death of one or the other. Early in the trip this might have taken place had it not been for an unwonted accident. At the end of this day they made a bleak and miserable camp on the shore of Lake Le Barge. Driving snow, a wind that cut like a white-hot knife, and darkness had forced them to grope for a camping place. They could hardly have fared worse. At their backs rose a perpendicular wall of rock, and Perrault and François were compelled to make their fire and spread their sleeping robes on the ice of the lake itself. The tent they had discarded at Dyea in order to travel light. A few sticks of driftwood furnished them with a fire that thawed down through the ice and left them to eat supper in the dark.

Close in under the sheltering rock Buck made his nest. So snug and warm was it, that he was loath to leave it when François distributed the fish which he had first thawed over the fire. But when Buck finished his ration and returned, he found his nest

515 occupied. A warning snarl told him that the trespasser was Spitz. Till now Buck had avoided trouble with his enemy, but this was too much. The beast in him roared. He sprang upon Spitz with a fury which surprised them both, and Spitz particularly, for his whole experience with Buck had gone to teach him that his rival was an unusually timid dog, who managed to hold his own only because of his great weight and size.

520 François was surprised, too, when they shot out in a tangle from the disrupted nest and he divined the cause of the trouble. "A-a-ah!" he cried to Buck. "Gif it to heem, by Gar! Gif it to heem, the dirty t'eef!"

Spitz was equally willing. He was crying with sheer rage and eagerness as he circled back and forth for a chance to spring in. Buck was no less eager, and no less

525 cautious, as he likewise circled back and forth for the advantage. But it was then that the unexpected happened, the thing which projected their struggle for supremacy far into the future, past many a weary mile of trail and toil.

An oath from Perrault, the resounding impact of a club upon a bony frame, and a shrill yelp of pain, heralded the breaking forth of pandemonium. The camp was

530 suddenly discovered to be alive with skulking furry forms,—starving huskies, four or five score of them, who had scented the camp from some Indian village. They had crept in while Buck and Spitz were fighting, and when the two men sprang among them with stout clubs they showed their teeth and fought back. They were crazed by the smell of the food. Perrault found one with head buried in the grub-box. His club handed heavily

535 on the gaunt ribs, and the grub-box was capsized on the ground. On the instant a score of the famished brutes were scrambling for the bread and bacon. The clubs fell upon them unheeded. They yelped and howled under the rain of blows, but struggled none the less madly till the last crumb had been devoured.

In the meantime the astonished team-dogs had burst out of their nests only to be

540 set upon by the fierce invaders. Never had Buck seen such dogs. It seemed as though their bones would burst through their skins. They were mere skeletons, draped loosely in draggled hides, with blazing eyes and slavered fangs. But the hunger-madness made them terrifying, irresistible. There was no opposing them. The team-dogs were swept back against the cliff at the first onset. Buck was beset by three huskies, and in a trice

545 his head and shoulders were ripped and slashed. The din was frightful. Billee was crying as usual. Dave and Sol-leks, dripping blood from a score of wounds, were fighting

bravely side by side. Joe was snapping like a demon. Once, his teeth closed on the fore leg of a husky, and he crunched down through the bone. Pike, the malingerer, leaped upon the crippled animal, breaking its neck with a quick flash of teeth and a jerk. Buck got a frothing adversary by the throat, and was sprayed with blood when his teeth sank through the jugular. The warm taste of it in his mouth goaded him to greater fierceness. He flung himself upon another, and at the same time felt teeth sink into his own throat. It was Spitz, treacherously attacking from the side.

Perrault and François, having cleaned out their part of the camp, hurried to save their sled-dogs. The wild wave of famished beasts rolled back before them, and Buck shook himself free. But it was only for a moment. The two men were compelled to run back to save the grub, upon which the huskies returned to the attack on the team. Billee, terrified into bravery, sprang through the savage circle and fled away over the ice. Pike and Dub followed on his heels, with the rest of the team behind. As Buck drew himself together to spring after them, out of the tail of his eye he saw Spitz rush upon him with the evident intention of overthrowing him. Once off his feet and under that mass of huskies, there was no hope for him. But he braced himself to the shock of Spitz's charge, then joined the flight out on the lake.

Later, the nine team-dogs gathered together and sought shelter in the forest. Though unpursued, they were in a sorry plight. There was not one who was not wounded in four or five places, while some were wounded grievously. Dub was badly injured in a hind leg; Dolly, the last husky added to the team at Dyea, had a badly torn throat; Joe had lost an eye; while Billee, the good-natured, with an ear chewed and rent to ribbons, cried and whimpered throughout the night. At daybreak they limped warily back to camp, to find the marauders gone and the two men in bad tempers. Fully half their grub supply was gone. The huskies had chewed through the sled lashings and canvas coverings. In fact, nothing, no matter how remotely eatable, had escaped them. They had eaten a pair of Perrault's moose-hide moccasins, chunks out of the leather traces, and even two feet of lash from the end of François's whip. He broke from a mournful contemplation of it to look over his wounded dogs.

"Ah, my frien's," he said softly, "mebbe it mek you mad dog, dose many bites. Mebbe all mad dog, sacredam! Wot you t'ink, eh, Perrault?"

The courier shook his head dubiously. With four hundred miles of trail still between him and Dawson, he could ill afford to have madness break out among his dogs. Two hours of cursing and exertion got the harnesses into shape, and the wound-stiffened team was under way, struggling painfully over the hardest part of the trail they had yet encountered, and for that matter, the hardest between them and Dawson.

The Thirty Mile River was wide open. Its wild water defied the frost, and it was in the eddies only and in the quiet places that the ice held at all. Six days of exhausting toil were required to cover those thirty terrible miles. And terrible they were, for every foot of them was accomplished at the risk of life to dog and man. A dozen times, Perrault, nosing the way, broke through the ice bridges, being saved by the long pole he carried, which he so held that it fell each time across the hole made by his body. But a cold snap was on, the thermometer registering fifty below zero, and each time he broke through he was compelled for very life to build a fire and dry his garments.

Nothing daunted him. It was because nothing daunted him that he had been chosen for government courier. He took all manner of risks, resolutely thrusting his little weazened face into the frost and struggling on from dim dawn to dark. He skirted the frowning shores on rim ice that bent and crackled under foot and upon which they dared not halt. Once, the sled broke through, with Dave and Buck, and they were half-frozen and all but drowned by the time they were dragged out. The usual fire was necessary to save them. They were coated solidly with ice, and the two men kept them on the run around the fire, sweating and thawing, so close that they were singed by the flames.

At another time Spitz went through, dragging the whole team after him up to Buck, who strained backward with all his strength, his fore paws on the slippery edge and the ice quivering and snapping all around. But behind him was Dave, likewise straining backward, and behind the sled was François, pulling till his tendons cracked.

Again, the rim ice broke away before and behind, and there was no escape except up the cliff. Perrault scaled it by a miracle, while François prayed for just that miracle; and with every thong and sled lashing and the last bit of harness rove into a long rope, the dogs were hoisted, one by one, to the cliff crest. François came up last, after the sled and load. Then came the search for a place to descend, which descent was ultimately made by the aid of the rope, and night found them back on the river with a quarter of a mile to the day's credit.

By the time they made the Hootalinqua and good ice, Buck was played out. The rest of the dogs were in like condition; but Perrault, to make up lost time, pushed them late and early. The first day they covered thirty-five miles to the Big Salmon; the next day thirty-five more to the Little Salmon; the third day forty miles, which brought them well up toward the Five Fingers.

Buck's feet were not so compact and hard as the feet of the huskies. His had softened during the many generations since the day his last wild ancestor was tamed by a cave-dweller or river man. All day long he limped in agony, and camp once made, lay down like a dead dog. Hungry as he was, he would not move to receive his ration of fish, which François had to bring to him. Also, the dog-driver rubbed Buck's feet for half an hour each night after supper, and sacrificed the tops of his own moccasins to make four moccasins for Buck. This was a great relief, and Buck caused even the weazened face of Perrault to twist itself into a grin one morning, when François forgot the moccasins and Buck lay on his back, his four feet waving appealingly in the air, and refused to budge without them. Later his feet grew hard to the trail, and the worn-out foot-gear was thrown away.

At the Pelly one morning, as they were harnessing up, Dolly, who had never been conspicuous for anything, went suddenly mad. She announced her condition by a long, heart-breaking wolf howl that sent every dog bristling with fear, then sprang straight for Buck. He had never seen a dog go mad, nor did he have any reason to fear madness; yet he knew that here was horror, and fled away from it in a panic. Straight away he raced, with Dolly, panting and frothing, one leap behind; nor could she gain on him, so great was his terror, nor could he leave her, so great was her madness. He plunged through the wooded breast of the island, flew down to the lower end, crossed a back channel filled with rough ice to another island, gained a third island, curved back to the main river, and in desperation started to cross it. And all the time, though he did not look, he could hear her snarling just one leap behind. François called to him a quarter of a mile away and he doubled back, still one leap ahead, gasping painfully for air and putting all his faith in that François would save him. The dog-driver held the axe poised in his hand, and as Buck shot past him the axe crashed down upon mad Dolly's head.

Buck staggered over against the sled, exhausted, sobbing for breath, helpless. This was Spitz's opportunity. He sprang upon Buck, and twice his teeth sank into his unresisting foe and ripped and tore the flesh to the bone. Then François's lash descended, and Buck had the satisfaction of watching Spitz receive the worst whipping as yet administered to any of the teams.

"One devil, dat Spitz," remarked Perrault. "Some dam day heem keel dat Buck."

"Dat Buck two devils," was François's rejoinder. "All de tam I watch dat Buck I know for sure. Lissen: some dam fine day heem get mad lak hell an' den heem chew dat Spitz all up an' spit heem out on de snow. Sure. I know."

From then on it was war between them. Spitz, as lead-dog and acknowledged master of the team, felt his supremacy threatened by this strange Southland dog. And strange Buck was to him, for of the many Southland dogs he had known, not one had shown up worthily in camp and on trail. They were all too soft, dying under the toil, the frost, and starvation. Buck was the exception. He alone endured and prospered, matching the husky in strength, savagery, and cunning. Then he was a masterful dog, and what made him dangerous was the fact that the club of the man in the red sweater had knocked all blind pluck and rashness out of his desire for mastery. He was preëminently cunning, and could bide his time with a patience that was nothing less than primitive.

It was inevitable that the clash for leadership should come. Buck wanted it. He wanted it because it was his nature, because he had been gripped tight by that nameless, incomprehensible pride of the trail and trace—that pride which holds dogs in the toil to the last gasp, which lures them to die joyfully in the harness, and breaks their hearts if they are cut out of the harness. This was the pride of Dave as wheel-dog, of Sol-leks as he pulled with all his strength; the pride that laid hold of them at break of camp, transforming them from sour and sullen brutes into straining, eager, ambitious creatures; the pride that spurred them on all day and dropped them at pitch of camp at night, letting them fall back into gloomy unrest and uncontent. This was the pride that bore up Spitz and made him thrash the sled-dogs who blundered and shirked in the traces or hid away at harness-up time in the morning. Likewise it was this pride that made him fear Buck as a possible lead-dog. And this was Buck's pride, too.

He openly threatened the other's leadership. He came between him and the shirks he should have punished. And he did it deliberately. One night there was a heavy snowfall, and in the morning Pike, the malingerer, did not appear. He was securely hidden in his nest under a foot of snow. François called him and sought him in vain. Spitz was wild with wrath. He raged through the camp, smelling and digging in every likely place, snarling so frightfully that Pike heard and shivered in his hiding-place.

But when he was at last unearthed, and Spitz flew at him to punish him, Buck flew, with equal rage, in between. So unexpected was it, and so shrewdly managed, that Spitz was hurled backward and off his feet. Pike, who had been trembling abjectly, took heart at this open mutiny, and sprang upon his overthrown leader. Buck, to whom fair play was a forgotten code, likewise sprang upon Spitz. But François, chuckling at the incident while unswerving in the administration of justice, brought his lash down upon Buck with all his might. This failed to drive Buck from his prostrate rival, and the butt of the whip was brought into play. Half-stunned by the blow, Buck was knocked backward and the lash laid upon him again and again, while Spitz soundly punished the many times offending Pike.

In the days that followed, as Dawson grew closer and closer, Buck still continued to interfere between Spitz and the culprits; but he did it craftily, when François was not around. With the covert mutiny of Buck, a general insubordination sprang up and increased. Dave and Sol-leks were unaffected, but the rest of the team went from bad to

690 worse. Things no longer went right. There was continual bickering and jangling. Trouble was always afoot, and at the bottom of it was Buck. He kept François busy, for the dog-driver was in constant apprehension of the life-and-death struggle between the two which he knew must take place sooner or later; and on more than one night the sounds of quarrelling and strife among the other dogs turned him out of his sleeping

695 robe, fearful that Buck and Spitz were at it.

But the opportunity did not present itself, and they pulled into Dawson one dreary afternoon with the great fight still to come. Here were many men, and countless dogs, and Buck found them all at work. It seemed the ordained order of things that dogs should work. All day they swung up and down the main street in long teams, and in the

700 night their jingling bells still went by. They hauled cabin logs and firewood, freighted up to the mines, and did all manner of work that horses did in the Santa Clara Valley. Here and there Buck met Southland dogs, but in the main they were the wild wolf husky breed. Every night, regularly, at nine, at twelve, at three, they lifted a nocturnal song, a weird and eerie chant, in which it was Buck's delight to join.

705 With the aurora borealis flaming coldly overhead, or the stars leaping in the frost dance, and the land numb and frozen under its pall of snow, this song of the huskies might have been the defiance of life, only it was pitched in minor key, with long-drawn wailings and half-sobs, and was more the pleading of life, the articulate travail of existence. It was an old song, old as the breed itself—one of the first songs of the

710 younger world in a day when songs were sad. It was invested with the woe of unnumbered generations, this plaint by which Buck was so strangely stirred. When he moaned and sobbed, it was with the pain of living that was of old the pain of his wild fathers, and the fear and mystery of the cold and dark that was to them fear and mystery. And that he should be stirred by it marked the completeness with which he harked back

715 through the ages of fire and roof to the raw beginnings of life in the howling ages.

Seven days from the time they pulled into Dawson, they dropped down the steep bank by the Barracks to the Yukon Trail, and pulled for Dyea and Salt Water. Perrault was carrying despatches if anything more urgent than those he had brought in; also, the travel pride had gripped him, and he purposed to make the record trip of the year.

720 Several things favored him in this. The week's rest had recuperated the dogs and put them in thorough trim. The trail they had broken into the country was packed hard by

later journeyers. And further, the police had arranged in two or three places deposits of grub for dog and man, and he was travelling light.

They made Sixty Mile, which is a fifty-mile run, on the first day; and the second day saw them booming up the Yukon well on their way to Pelly. But such splendid running was achieved not without great trouble and vexation on the part of François. The insidious revolt led by Buck had destroyed the solidarity of the team. It no longer was as one dog leaping in the traces. The encouragement Buck gave the rebels led them into all kinds of petty misdemeanors. No more was Spitz a leader greatly to be feared. The old awe departed, and they grew equal to challenging his authority. Pike robbed him of half a fish one night, and gulped it down under the protection of Buck. Another night Dub and Joe fought Spitz and made him forego the punishment they deserved. And even Billee, the good-natured, was less good-natured, and whined not half so placatingly as in former days. Buck never came near Spitz without snarling and bristling menacingly. In fact, his conduct approached that of a bully, and he was given to swaggering up and down before Spitz's very nose.

The breaking down of discipline likewise affected the dogs in their relations with one another. They quarrelled and bickered more than ever among themselves, till at times the camp was a howling bedlam. Dave and Sol-leks alone were unaltered, though they were made irritable by the unending squabbling. François swore strange barbarous oaths, and stamped the snow in futile rage, and tore his hair. His lash was always singing among the dogs, but it was of small avail. Directly his back was turned they were at it again. He backed up Spitz with his whip, while Buck backed up the remainder of the team. François knew he was behind all the trouble, and Buck knew he knew; but Buck was too clever ever again to be caught red-handed. He worked faithfully in the harness, for the toil had become a delight to him; yet it was a greater delight slyly to precipitate a fight amongst his mates and tangle the traces.

At the mouth of the Tahkeena, one night after supper, Dub turned up a snowshoe rabbit, blundered it, and missed. In a second the whole team was in full cry. A hundred yards away was a camp of the Northwest Police, with fifty dogs, huskies all, who joined the chase. The rabbit sped down the river, turned off into a small creek, up the frozen bed of which it held steadily. It ran lightly on the surface of the snow, while the dogs ploughed through by main strength. Buck led the pack, sixty strong, around bend after bend, but he could not gain. He lay down low to the race, whining eagerly, his splendid body flashing forward, leap by leap, in the wan white moonlight. And leap by leap, like some pale frost wraith, the snowshoe rabbit flashed on ahead.

All that stirring of old instincts which at stated periods drives men out from the sounding cities to forest and plain to kill things by chemically propelled leaden pellets, the blood lust, the joy to kill—all this was Buck's, only it was infinitely more intimate. He was ranging at the head of the pack, running the wild thing down, the living meat, to kill with his own teeth and wash his muzzle to the eyes in warm blood.

There is an ecstasy that marks the summit of life, and beyond which life cannot rise. And such is the paradox of living, this ecstasy comes when one is most alive, and it comes as a complete forgetfulness that one is alive. This ecstasy, this forgetfulness of living, comes to the artist, caught up and out of himself in a sheet of flame; it comes to the soldier, war-mad on a stricken field and refusing quarter; and it came to Buck, leading the pack, sounding the old wolf-cry, straining after the food that was alive and that fled swiftly before him through the moonlight. He was sounding the deeps of his nature, and of the parts of his nature that were deeper than he, going back into the womb of Time. He was mastered by the sheer surging of life, the tidal wave of being, the perfect joy of each separate muscle, joint, and sinew in that it was everything that was not death, that it was aglow and rampant, expressing itself in movement, flying exultantly under the stars and over the face of dead matter that did not move.

But Spitz, cold and calculating even in his supreme moods, left the pack and cut across a narrow neck of land where the creek made a long bend around. Buck did not know of this, and as he rounded the bend, the frost wraith of a rabbit still flitting before him, he saw another and larger frost wraith leap from the overhanging bank into the immediate path of the rabbit. It was Spitz. The rabbit could not turn, and as the white teeth broke its back in mid air it shrieked as loudly as a stricken man may shriek. At sound of this, the cry of Life plunging down from Life's apex in the grip of Death, the full pack at Buck's heels raised a hell's chorus of delight.

Buck did not cry out. He did not check himself, but drove in upon Spitz, shoulder to shoulder, so hard that he missed the throat. They rolled over and over in the powdery snow. Spitz gained his feet almost as though he had not been overthrown, slashing Buck down the shoulder and leaping clear. Twice his teeth clipped together, like the steel jaws of a trap, as he backed away for better footing, with lean and lifting lips that writhed and snarled.

In a flash Buck knew it. The time had come. It was to the death. As they circled about, snarling, ears laid back, keenly watchful for the advantage, the scene came to Buck with a sense of familiarity. He seemed to remember it all,—the white woods, and earth, and moonlight, and the thrill of battle. Over the whiteness and silence brooded a ghostly calm. There was not the faintest whisper of air—nothing moved, not a leaf quivered, the visible breaths of the dogs rising slowly and lingering in the frosty air. They had made short work of the snowshoe rabbit, these dogs that were ill-tamed wolves; and

795 they were now drawn up in an expectant circle. They, too, were silent, their eyes only gleaming and their breaths drifting slowly upward. To Buck it was nothing new or strange, this scene of old time. It was as though it had always been, the wonted way of things.

Spitz was a practised fighter. From Spitzbergen through the Arctic, and across

800 Canada and the Barrens, he had held his own with all manner of dogs and achieved to mastery over them. Bitter rage was his, but never blind rage. In passion to rend and destroy, he never forgot that his enemy was in like passion to rend and destroy. He never rushed till he was prepared to receive a rush; never attacked till he had first defended that attack.

805 In vain Buck strove to sink his teeth in the neck of the big white dog. Wherever his fangs struck for the softer flesh, they were countered by the fangs of Spitz. Fang clashed fang, and lips were cut and bleeding, but Buck could not penetrate his enemy's guard. Then he warmed up and enveloped Spitz in a whirlwind of rushes. Time and time again he tried for the snow-white throat, where life bubbled near to the surface, and

810 each time and every time Spitz slashed him and got away. Then Buck took to rushing, as though for the throat, when, suddenly drawing back his head and curving in from the side, he would drive his shoulder at the shoulder of Spitz, as a ram by which to overthrow him. But instead, Buck's shoulder was slashed down each time as Spitz leaped lightly away.

815 Spitz was untouched, while Buck was streaming with blood and panting hard. The fight was growing desperate. And all the while the silent and wolfish circle waited to finish off whichever dog went down. As Buck grew winded, Spitz took to rushing, and he kept him staggering for footing. Once Buck went over, and the whole circle of sixty dogs started up; but he recovered himself, almost in mid air, and the circle sank down again

820 and waited.

But Buck possessed a quality that made for greatness—imagination. He fought by instinct, but he could fight by head as well. He rushed, as though attempting the old shoulder trick, but at the last instant swept low to the snow and in. His teeth closed on Spitz's left fore leg. There was a crunch of breaking bone, and the white dog faced him

825 on three legs. Thrice he tried to knock him over, then repeated the trick and broke the right fore leg. Despite the pain and helplessness, Spitz struggled madly to keep up. He

saw the silent circle, with gleaming eyes, lolling tongues, and silvery breaths drifting upward, closing in upon him as he had seen similar circles close in upon beaten antagonists in the past. Only this time he was the one who was beaten.

830   There was no hope for him. Buck was inexorable. Mercy was a thing reserved for gentler climes. He manœuvred for the final rush. The circle had tightened till he could feel the breaths of the huskies on his flanks. He could see them, beyond Spitz and to either side, half crouching for the spring, their eyes fixed upon him. A pause seemed to fall. Every animal was motionless as though turned to stone. Only Spitz quivered and

835 bristled as he staggered back and forth, snarling with horrible menace, as though to frighten off impending death. Then Buck sprang in and out; but while he was in, shoulder had at last squarely met shoulder. The dark circle became a dot on the moon-flooded snow as Spitz disappeared from view. Buck stood and looked on, the successful champion, the dominant primordial beast who had made his kill and found it

840 good.

CHAPTER FOUR

Who Has Won to Mastership

$\mathcal{E}$H? W OT I say? I spik true w'en I say dat Buck two devils."

This was François's speech next morning when he discovered Spitz missing and Buck covered with wounds. He drew him to the fire and by its light pointed them out.

"Dat Spitz fight lak hell," said Perrault, as he surveyed the gaping rips and cuts.

845 "An' dat Buck fight lak two hells," was François's answer. "An' now we make good time. No more Spitz, no more trouble, sure."

While Perrault packed the camp outfit and loaded the sled, the dog-driver proceeded to harness the dogs. Buck trotted up to the place Spitz would have occupied as leader; but François, not noticing him, brought Sol-leks to the coveted position. In his judgment, Sol-leks was the best lead-dog left. Buck sprang upon Sol-leks in a fury, driving him back and standing in his place.

"Eh? eh?" François cried, slapping his thighs gleefully. "Look at dat Buck. Heem keel dat Spitz, heem t'ink to take de job."

"Go 'way, Chook!" he cried, but Buck refused to budge.

855 He took Buck by the scruff of the neck, and though the dog growled threateningly, dragged him to one side and replaced Sol-leks. The old dog did not like it, and showed plainly that he was afraid of Buck. François was obdurate, but when he turned his back Buck again displaced Sol-leks, who was not at all unwilling to go.

François was angry. "Now, by Gar, I feex you!" he cried, coming back with a
heavy club in his hand.

Buck remembered the man in the red sweater, and retreated slowly; nor did he
attempt to charge in when Sol-leks was once more brought forward. But he circled just
beyond the range of the club, snarling with bitterness and rage; and while he circled he
watched the club so as to dodge it if thrown by François, for he was become wise in the
way of clubs.

The driver went about his work, and he called to Buck when he was ready to put
him in his old place in front of Dave. Buck retreated two or three steps. François
followed him up, whereupon he again retreated. After some time of this, François threw
down the club, thinking that Buck feared a thrashing. But Buck was in open revolt. He
wanted, not to escape a clubbing, but to have the leadership. It was his by right. He had
earned it, and he would not be content with less.

Perrault took a hand. Between them they ran him about for the better part of an
hour. They threw clubs at him. He dodged. They cursed him, and his fathers and
mothers before him, and all his seed to come after him down to the remotest generation,
and every hair on his body and drop of blood in his veins; and he answered curse with
snarl and kept out of their reach. He did not try to run away, but retreated around and
around the camp, advertising plainly that when his desire was met, he would come in and
be good.

François sat down and scratched his head. Perrault looked at his watch and
swore. Time was flying, and they should have been on the trail an hour gone. François
scratched his head again. He shook it and grinned sheepishly at the courier, who
shrugged his shoulders in sign that they were beaten. Then François went up to where
Sol-leks stood and called to Buck. Buck laughed, as dogs laugh, yet kept his distance.
François unfastened Sol-leks's traces and put him back in his old place. The team stood
harnessed to the sled in an unbroken line, ready for the trail. There was no place for
Buck save at the front. Once more François called, and once more Buck laughed and
kept away.

"T'row down de club," Perrault commanded.

François complied, whereupon Buck trotted in, laughing triumphantly, and swung
around into position at the head of the team. His traces were fastened, the sled broken
out, and with both men running they dashed out on to the river trail.

Highly as the dog-driver had forevalued Buck, with his two devils, he found, while the day was yet young, that he had undervalued. At a bound Buck took up the duties of leadership; and where judgment was required, and quick thinking and quick acting, he

895 showed himself the superior even of Spitz, of whom François had never seen an equal.

But it was in giving the law and making his mates live up to it, that Buck excelled. Dave and Sol-leks did not mind the change in leadership. It was none of their business. Their business was to toil, and toil mightily, in the traces. So long as that were not interfered with, they did not care what happened. Billee, the good-natured, could lead

900 for all they cared, so long as he kept order. The rest of the team, however, had grown unruly during the last days of Spitz, and their surprise was great now that Buck proceeded to lick them into shape.

Pike, who pulled at Buck's heels, and who never put an ounce more of his weight against the breast-band than he was compelled to do, was swiftly and repeatedly shaken

905 for loafing; and ere the first day was done he was pulling more than ever before in his life. The first night in camp, Joe, the sour one, was punished roundly—a thing that Spitz had never succeeded in doing. Buck simply smothered him by virtue of superior weight, and cut him up till he ceased snapping and began to whine for mercy.

The general tone of the team picked up immediately. It recovered its old-time

910 solidarity, and once more the dogs leaped as one dog in the traces. At the Rink Rapids two native huskies, Teek and Koona, were added; and the celerity with which Buck broke them in took away François's breath.

"Nevaire such a dog as dat Buck!" he cried. "No, nevaire! Heem worth one t'ousan' dollair, by Gar! Eh? Wot you say, Perrault?"

915 And Perrault nodded. He was ahead of the record then, and gaining day by day. The trail was in excellent condition, well packed and hard, and there was no new-fallen snow with which to contend. It was not too cold. The temperature dropped to fifty below zero and remained there the whole trip. The men rode and ran by turn, and the dogs were kept on the jump, with but infrequent stoppages.

920 The Thirty Mile River was comparatively coated with ice, and they covered in one day going out what had taken them ten days coming in. In one run they made a sixty-mile dash from the foot of Lake Le Barge to the White Horse Rapids. Across Marsh, Tagish, and Bennett (seventy miles of lakes), they flew so fast that the man whose turn it was to run towed behind the sled at the end of a rope. And on the last night of

925 the second week they topped White Pass and dropped down the sea slope with the lights of Skaguay and of the shipping at their feet.

It was a record run. Each day for fourteen days they had averaged forty miles.

For three days Perrault and François threw chests up and down the main street of
Skaguay and were deluged with invitations to drink, while the team was the constant
930 centre of a worshipful crowd of dog-busters and mushers. Then three or four western
bad men aspired to clean out the town, were riddled like pepper-boxes for their pains,
and public interest turned to other idols. Next came official orders. François called
Buck to him, threw his arms around him, wept over him. And that was the last of
François and Perrault. Like other men, they passed out of Buck's life for good.

935 A Scotch half-breed took charge of him and his mates, and in company with a
dozen other dog-teams he started back over the weary trail to Dawson. It was no light
running now, nor record time, but heavy toil each day, with a heavy load behind; for this
was the mail train, carrying word from the world to the men who sought gold under the
shadow of the Pole.

940 Buck did not like it, but he bore up well to the work, taking pride in it after the
manner of Dave and Sol-leks, and seeing that his mates, whether they prided in it or not,
did their fair share. It was a monotonous life, operating with machine-like regularity.
One day was very like another. At a certain time each morning the cooks turned out,
fires were built, and breakfast was eaten. Then, while some broke camp, others
945 harnessed the dogs, and they were under way an hour or so before the darkness fell
which gave warning of dawn. At night, camp was made. Some pitched the flies, others
cut firewood and pine boughs for the beds, and still others carried water or ice for the
cooks. Also, the dogs were fed. To them, this was the one feature of the day, though it
was good to loaf around, after the fish was eaten, for an hour or so with the other dogs,
950 of which there were fivescore and odd. There were fierce fighters among them, but
three battles with the fiercest brought Buck to mastery, so that when he bristled and
showed his teeth they got out of his way.

Best of all, perhaps, he loved to lie near the fire, hind legs crouched under him,
fore legs stretched out in front, head raised, and eyes blinking dreamily at the flames.
955 Sometimes he thought of Judge Miller's big house in the sun-kissed Santa Clara Valley,
and of the cement swimming-tank, and Ysabel, the Mexican hairless, and Toots, the
Japanese pug; but oftener he remembered the man in the red sweater, the death of
Curly, the great fight with Spitz, and the good things he had eaten or would like to eat.
He was not homesick. The Sunland was very dim and distant, and such memories had
960 no power over him. Far more potent were the memories of his heredity that gave things
he had never seen before a seeming familiarity; the instincts (which were but the
memories of his ancestors become habits) which had lapsed in later days, and still later,

in him, quickened and become alive again.

Sometimes as he crouched there, blinking dreamily at the flames, it seemed that the flames were of another fire, and that as he crouched by this other fire he saw another and different man from the half-breed cook before him. This other man was shorter of leg and longer of arm, with muscles that were stringy and knotty rather than rounded and swelling. The hair of this man was long and matted, and his head slanted back under it from the eyes. He uttered strange sounds, and seemed very much afraid of the darkness, into which he peered continually, clutching in his hand, which hung midway between knee and foot, a stick with a heavy stone made fast to the end. He was all but naked, a ragged and fire-scorched skin hanging part way down his back, but on his body there was much hair. In some places, across the chest and shoulders and down the outside of the arms and thighs, it was matted into almost a thick fur. He did not stand erect, but with trunk inclined forward from the hips, on legs that bent at the knees. About his body there was a peculiar springiness, or resiliency, almost catlike, and a quick alertness as of one who lived in perpetual fear of things seen and unseen.

At other times this hairy man squatted by the fire with head between his legs and slept. On such occasions his elbows were on his knees, his hands clasped above his head as though to shed rain by the hairy arms. And beyond that fire, in the circling darkness, Buck could see many gleaming coals, two by two, always two by two, which he knew to be the eyes of great beasts of prey. And he could hear the crashing of their bodies through the undergrowth, and the noises they made in the night. And dreaming there by the Yukon bank, with lazy eyes blinking at the fire, these sounds and sights of another world would make the hair to rise along his back and stand on end across his shoulders and up his neck, till he whimpered low and suppressedly, or growled softly, and the half-breed cook shouted at him, "Hey, you Buck, wake up!" Whereupon the other world would vanish and the real world come into his eyes, and he would get up and yawn and stretch as though he had been asleep.

It was a hard trip, with the mail behind them, and the heavy work wore them down. They were short of weight and in poor condition when they made Dawson, and should have had a ten days' or a week's rest at least. But in two days' time they dropped down the Yukon bank from the Barracks, loaded with letters for the outside. The dogs were tired, the drivers grumbling, and to make matters worse, it snowed every day. This meant a soft trail, greater friction on the runners, and heavier pulling for the dogs; yet the drivers were fair through it all, and did their best for the animals.

Each night the dogs were attended to first. They ate before the drivers ate, and no man sought his sleeping-robe till he had seen to the feet of the dogs he drove. Still, their strength went down. Since the beginning of the winter they had travelled eighteen hundred miles, dragging sleds the whole weary distance; and eighteen hundred miles will tell upon life of the toughest. Buck stood it, keeping his mates up to their work and maintaining discipline, though he, too, was very tired. Billee cried and whimpered regularly in his sleep each night. Joe was sourer than ever, and Sol-leks was unapproachable, blind side or other side.

But it was Dave who suffered most of all. Something had gone wrong with him. He became more morose and irritable, and when camp was pitched at once made his nest, where his driver fed him. Once out of the harness and down, he did not get on his feet again till harness-up time in the morning. Sometimes, in the traces, when jerked by a sudden stoppage of the sled, or by straining to start it, he would cry out with pain. The driver examined him, but could find nothing. All the drivers became interested in his case. They talked it over at meal-time, and over their last pipes before going to bed, and one night they held a consultation. He was brought from his nest to the fire and was pressed and prodded till he cried out many times. Something was wrong inside, but they could locate no broken bones, could not make it out.

By the time Cassiar Bar was reached, he was so weak that he was falling repeatedly in the traces. The Scotch half-breed called a halt and took him out of the team, making the next dog, Sol-leks, fast to the sled. His intention was to rest Dave, letting him run free behind the sled. Sick as he was, Dave resented being taken out, grunting and growling while the traces were unfastened, and whimpering broken-heartedly when he saw Sol-leks in the position he had held and served so long. For the pride of trace and trail was his, and, sick unto death, he could not bear that another dog should do his work.

When the sled started, he floundered in the soft snow alongside the beaten trail, attacking Sol-leks with his teeth, rushing against him and trying to thrust him off into the soft snow on the other side, striving to leap inside his traces and get between him and the sled, and all the while whining and yelping and crying with grief and pain. The half-breed tried to drive him away with the whip; but he paid no heed to the stinging lash, and the man had not the heart to strike harder. Dave refused to run quietly on the trail behind the sled, where the going was easy, but continued to flounder alongside in the soft snow, where the going was most difficult, till exhausted. Then he fell, and lay where he fell, howling lugubriously as the long train of sleds churned by.

With the last remnant of his strength he managed to stagger along behind till the train made another stop, when he floundered past the sleds to his own, where he stood alongside Sol-leks. His driver lingered a moment to get a light for his pipe from the man behind. Then he returned and started his dogs. They swung out on the trail with remarkable lack of exertion, turned their heads uneasily, and stopped in surprise. The driver was surprised, too; the sled had not moved. He called his comrades to witness the sight. Dave had bitten through both of Sol-leks's traces, and was standing directly in front of the sled in his proper place.

He pleaded with his eyes to remain there. The driver was perplexed. His comrades talked of how a dog could break its heart through being denied the work that killed it, and recalled instances they had known, where dogs, too old for the toil, or injured, had died because they were cut out of the traces. Also, they held it a mercy, since Dave was to die anyway, that he should die in the traces, heart-easy and content. So he was harnessed in again, and proudly he pulled as of old, though more than once he cried out involuntarily from the bite of his inward hurt. Several times he fell down and was dragged in the traces, and once the sled ran upon him so that he limped thereafter in one of his hind legs.

But he held out till camp was reached, when his driver made a place for him by the fire. Morning found him too weak to travel. At harness-up time he tried to crawl to his driver. By convulsive efforts he got on his feet, staggered, and fell. Then he wormed his way forward slowly toward where the harnesses were being put on his mates. He would advance his fore legs and drag up his body with a sort of hitching movement, when he would advance his fore legs and hitch ahead again for a few more inches. His strength left him, and the last his mates saw of him he lay gasping in the snow and yearning toward them. But they could hear him mournfully howling till they passed out of sight behind a belt of river timber.

Here the train was halted. The Scotch half-breed slowly retraced his steps to the camp they had left. The men ceased talking. A revolver-shot rang out. The man came back hurriedly. The whips snapped, the bells tinkled merrily, the sleds churned along the trail; but Buck knew, and every dog knew, what had taken place behind the belt of river trees.

CHAPTER FIVE

The Toil of Trace and Trail

THIRTY DAYS FROM the time it left Dawson, the Salt Water Mail, with Buck and his mates at the fore, arrived at Skaguay. They were in a wretched state, worn out and worn down. Buck's one hundred and forty pounds had dwindled to one hundred and fifteen. The rest of his mates, though lighter dogs, had relatively lost more weight than he. Pike, the malingerer, who, in his lifetime of deceit, had often successfully feigned a hurt leg, was now limping in earnest. Sol-leks was limping, and Dub was suffering from a wrenched shoulder-blade.

They were all terribly footsore. No spring or rebound was left in them. Their feet fell heavily on the trail, jarring their bodies and doubling the fatigue of a day's travel. There was nothing the matter with them except that they were dead tired. It was not the dead-tiredness that comes through brief and excessive effort, from which recovery is a matter of hours; but it was the dead-tiredness that comes through the slow and prolonged strength drainage of months of toil. There was no power of recuperation left, no reserve strength to call upon. It had been all used, the last least bit of it. Every muscle, every fibre, every cell, was tired, dead tired. And there was reason for it. In less than five months they had travelled twenty-five hundred miles, during the last eighteen hundred of which they had had but five days' rest. When they arrived at Skaguay they were apparently on their last legs. They could barely keep the traces taut, and on the down grades just managed to keep out of the way of the sled.

"Mush on, poor sore feets," the driver encouraged them as they tottered down the main street of Skaguay. "Dis is de las'. Den we get one long res'. Eh? For sure. One bully long res'."

1085 The drivers confidently expected a long stopover. Themselves, they had covered twelve hundred miles with two days' rest, and in the nature of reason and common justice they deserved an interval of loafing. But so many were the men who had rushed into the Klondike, and so many were the sweethearts, wives, and kin that had not rushed in, that the congested mail was taking on Alpine proportions; also, there were official

1090 orders. Fresh batches of Hudson Bay dogs were to take the places of those worthless for the trail. The worthless ones were to be got rid of, and, since dogs count for little against dollars, they were to be sold.

Three days passed, by which time Buck and his mates found how really tired and weak they were. Then, on the morning of the fourth day, two men from the States came

1095 along and bought them, harness and all, for a song. The men addressed each other as "Hal" and "Charles." Charles was a middle-aged, lightish-colored man, with weak and watery eyes and a mustache that twisted fiercely and vigorously up, giving the lie to the limply drooping lip it concealed. Hal was a youngster of nineteen or twenty, with a big Colt's revolver and a hunting-knife strapped about him on a belt that fairly bristled with

1100 cartridges. This belt was the most salient thing about him. It advertised his callowness—a callowness sheer and unutterable. Both men were manifestly out of place, and why such as they should adventure the North is part of the mystery of things that passes understanding.

Buck heard the chaffering, saw the money pass between the man and the

1105 Government agent, and knew that the Scotch half-breed and the mail-train drivers were passing out of his life on the heels of Perrault and François and the others who had gone before. When driven with his mates to the new owners' camp, Buck saw a slipshod and slovenly affair, tent half stretched, dishes unwashed, everything in disorder; also, he saw a woman. "Mercedes" the men called her. She was Charles's wife and Hal's sister—a nice

1110 family party.

Buck watched them apprehensively as they proceeded to take down the tent and load the sled. There was a great deal of effort about their manner, but no businesslike method. The tent was rolled into an awkward bundle three times as large as it should have been. The tin dishes were packed away unwashed. Mercedes continually fluttered

1115 in the way of her men and kept up an unbroken chattering of remonstrance and advice. When they put a clothes-sack on the front of the sled, she suggested it should go on the back; and when they had put it on the back, and covered it over with a couple of other bundles, she discovered overlooked articles which could abide nowhere else but in that very sack, and they unloaded again.

1120 Three men from a neighboring tent came out and looked on, grinning and winking at one another.

"You've got a right smart load as it is," said one of them; "and it's not me should tell you your business, but I wouldn't tote that tent along if I was you."

"Undreamed of!" cried Mercedes, throwing up her hands in dainty dismay.
1125 "However in the world could I manage without a tent?"

"It's springtime, and you won't get any more cold weather," the man replied.

She shook her head decidedly, and Charles and Hal put the last odds and ends on top the mountainous load.

"Think it'll ride?" one of the men asked.

1130 "Why shouldn't it?" Charles demanded rather shortly.

"Oh, that's all right, that's all right," the man hastened meekly to say. "I was just a-wonderin', that is all. It seemed a mite top-heavy."

Charles turned his back and drew the lashings down as well as he could, which was not in the least well.

1135 "An' of course the dogs can hike along all day with that contraption behind them," affirmed a second of the men.

"Certainly," said Hal, with freezing politeness, taking hold of the gee-pole with one hand and swinging his whip from the other. "Mush!" he shouted. "Mush on there!"

The dogs sprang against the breast-bands, strained hard for a few moments, then
1140 relaxed. They were unable to move the sled.

"The lazy brutes, I'll show them," he cried, preparing to lash out at them with the whip.

But Mercedes interfered, crying, "Oh, Hal, you mustn't," as she caught hold of the whip and wrenched it from him. "The poor dears! Now you must promise you won't be
1145 harsh with them for the rest of the trip, or I won't go a step."

"Precious lot you know about dogs," her brother sneered; "and I wish you'd leave me alone. They're lazy, I tell you, and you've got to whip them to get anything out of them. That's their way. You ask any one. Ask one of those men."

Mercedes looked at them imploringly, untold repugnance at sight of pain written
1150 in her pretty face.

"They're weak as water, if you want to know," came the reply from one of the men. "Plum tuckered out, that's what's the matter. They need a rest."

"Rest be blanked," said Hal, with his beardless lips; and Mercedes said, "Oh!" in pain and sorrow at the oath.

1155 But she was a clannish creature, and rushed at once to the defence of her brother. "Never mind that man," she said pointedly. "You're driving our dogs, and you do what you think best with them."

Again Hal's whip fell upon the dogs. They threw themselves against the breast-bands, dug their feet into the packed snow, got down low to it, and put forth all 1160 their strength. The sled held as though it were an anchor. After two efforts, they stood still, panting. The whip was whistling savagely, when once more Mercedes interfered. She dropped on her knees before Buck, with tears in her eyes, and put her arms around his neck.

"You poor, poor dears," she cried sympathetically, "why don't you pull hard?—then 1165 you wouldn't be whipped." Buck did not like her, but he was feeling too miserable to resist her, taking it as part of the day's miserable work.

One of the onlookers, who had been clenching his teeth to suppress hot speech, now spoke up:—

"It's not that I care a whoop what becomes of you, but for the dogs' sakes I just 1170 want to tell you, you can help them a mighty lot by breaking out that sled. The runners are froze fast. Throw your weight against the gee-pole, right and left, and break it out."

A third time the attempt was made, but this time, following the advice, Hal broke out the runners which had been frozen to the snow. The overloaded and unwieldy sled forged ahead, Buck and his mates struggling frantically under the rain of blows. A 1175 hundred yards ahead the path turned and sloped steeply into the main street. It would have required an experienced man to keep the top-heavy sled upright, and Hal was not such a man. As they swung on the turn the sled went over, spilling half its load through the loose lashings. The dogs never stopped. The lightened sled bounded on its side behind them. They were angry because of the ill treatment they had received and the 1180 unjust load. Buck was raging. He broke into a run, the team following his lead. Hal cried "Whoa! whoa!" but they gave no heed. He tripped and was pulled off his feet. The capsized sled ground over him, and the dogs dashed on up the street, adding to the gayety of Skaguay as they scattered the remainder of the outfit along its chief thoroughfare.

1185 Kind-hearted citizens caught the dogs and gathered up the scattered belongings. Also, they gave advice. Half the load and twice the dogs, if they ever expected to reach Dawson, was what was said. Hal and his sister and brother-in-law listened unwillingly, pitched tent, and overhauled the outfit. Canned goods were turned out that made men laugh, for canned goods on the Long Trail is a thing to dream about. "Blankets for a hotel," quoth one of the men who laughed and helped. "Half as many is too much; get rid of them. Throw away that tent, and all those dishes,—who's going to wash them, anyway? Good Lord, do you think you're travelling on a Pullman?"

And so it went, the inexorable elimination of the superfluous. Mercedes cried when her clothes-bags were dumped on the ground and article after article was thrown out. She cried in general, and she cried in particular over each discarded thing. She clasped hands about knees, rocking back and forth broken-heartedly. She averred she would not go an inch, not for a dozen Charleses. She appealed to everybody and to everything, finally wiping her eyes and proceeding to cast out even articles of apparel that were imperative necessaries. And in her zeal, when she had finished with her own, she attacked the belongings of her men and went through them like a tornado.

This accomplished, the outfit, though cut in half, was still a formidable bulk. Charles and Hal went out in the evening and bought six Outside dogs. These, added to the six of the original team, and Teek and Koona, the huskies obtained at the Rink Rapids on the record trip, brought the team up to fourteen. But the Outside dogs, though practically broken in since their landing, did not amount to much. Three were short-haired pointers, one was a Newfoundland, and the other two were mongrels of indeterminate breed. They did not seem to know anything, these newcomers. Buck and his comrades looked upon them with disgust, and though he speedily taught them their places and what not to do, he could not teach them what to do. They did not take kindly to trace and trail. With the exception of the two mongrels, they were bewildered and spirit-broken by the strange savage environment in which they found themselves and by the ill-treatment they had received. The two mongrels were without spirit at all; bones were the only things breakable about them.

With the newcomers hopeless and forlorn, and the old team worn out by twenty-five hundred miles of continuous trail, the outlook was anything but bright. The two men, however, were quite cheerful. And they were proud, too. They were doing the thing in style, with fourteen dogs. They had seen other sleds depart over the Pass for Dawson, or come in from Dawson, but never had they seen a sled with so many as fourteen dogs. In the nature of Arctic travel there was a reason why fourteen dogs should not drag one sled, and that was that one sled could not carry the food for fourteen dogs. But Charles and Hal did not know this. They had worked the trip out with a pencil, so much to a dog, so many dogs, so many days, Q.E.D. Mercedes looked over their shoulders and nodded comprehensively, it was all so very simple.

Late next morning Buck led the long team up the street. There was nothing lively about it, no snap or go in him and his fellows. They were starting dead weary. Four times he had covered the distance between Salt Water and Dawson, and the knowledge that, jaded and tired, he was facing the same trail once more, made him bitter. His heart was not in the work, nor was the heart of any dog. The Outsides were timid and frightened, the Insides without confidence in their masters.

Buck felt vaguely that there was no depending upon these two men and the woman. They did not know how to do anything, and as the days went by it became apparent that they could not learn. They were slack in all things, without order or discipline. It took them half the night to pitch a slovenly camp, and half the morning to break that camp and get the sled loaded in fashion so slovenly that for the rest of the day they were occupied in stopping and rearranging the load. Some days they did not make ten miles. On other days they were unable to get started at all. And on no day did they succeed in making more than half the distance used by the men as a basis in their dog-food computation.

It was inevitable that they should go short on dog-food. But they hastened it by overfeeding, bringing the day nearer when underfeeding would commence. The Outside dogs, whose digestions had not been trained by chronic famine to make the most of little, had voracious appetites. And when, in addition to this, the worn-out huskies pulled weakly, Hal decided that the orthodox ration was too small. He doubled it. And to cap it all, when Mercedes, with tears in her pretty eyes and a quaver in her throat, could not cajole him into giving the dogs still more, she stole from the fish-sacks and fed them slyly. But it was not food that Buck and the huskies needed, but rest. And though they were making poor time, the heavy load they dragged sapped their strength severely.

Then came the underfeeding. Hal awoke one day to the fact that his dog-food was half gone and the distance only quarter covered; further, that for love or money no additional dog-food was to be obtained. So he cut down even the orthodox ration and tried to increase the day's travel. His sister and brother-in-law seconded him; but they were frustrated by their heavy outfit and their own incompetence. It was a simple matter to give the dogs less food; but it was impossible to make the dogs travel faster, while their own inability to get under way earlier in the morning prevented them from travelling longer hours. Not only did they not know how to work dogs, but they did not know how to work themselves.

The first to go was Dub. Poor blundering thief that he was, always getting caught and punished, he had none the less been a faithful worker. His wrenched shoulder-blade, untreated and unrested, went from bad to worse, till finally Hal shot him with the big Colt's revolver. It is a saying of the country that an Outside dog starves to death on the ration of the husky, so the six Outside dogs under Buck could do no less than die on half the ration of the husky. The Newfoundland went first, followed by the three short-haired pointers, the two mongrels hanging more grittily on to life, but going in the end.

By this time all the amenities and gentlenesses of the Southland had fallen away from the three people. Shorn of its glamour and romance, Arctic travel became to them a reality too harsh for their manhood and womanhood. Mercedes ceased weeping over the dogs, being too occupied with weeping over herself and with quarrelling with her husband and brother. To quarrel was the one thing they were never too weary to do. Their irritability arose out of their misery, increased with it, doubled upon it, outdistanced it. The wonderful patience of the trail which comes to men who toil hard and suffer sore, and remain sweet of speech and kindly, did not come to these two men and the woman. They had no inkling of such a patience. They were stiff and in pain; their muscles ached, their bones ached, their very hearts ached; and because of this they became sharp of speech, and hard words were first on their lips in the morning and last at night.

Charles and Hal wrangled whenever Mercedes gave them a chance. It was the cherished belief of each that he did more than his share of the work, and neither forbore to speak this belief at every opportunity. Sometimes Mercedes sided with her husband, sometimes with her brother. The result was a beautiful and unending family quarrel. Starting from a dispute as to which should chop a few sticks for the fire (a dispute which concerned only Charles and Hal), presently would be lugged in the rest of the family, fathers, mothers, uncles, cousins, people thousands of miles away, and some of them dead. That Hal's views on art, or the sort of society plays his mother's brother wrote, should have anything to do with the chopping of a few sticks of firewood, passes comprehension; nevertheless the quarrel was as likely to tend in that direction as in the direction of Charles's political prejudices. And that Charles's sister's tale-bearing tongue should be relevant to the building of a Yukon fire, was apparent only to Mercedes, who disburdened herself of copious opinions upon that topic, and incidentally upon a few other traits unpleasantly peculiar to her husband's family. In the meantime the fire remained unbuilt, the camp half pitched, and the dogs unfed.

Mercedes nursed a special grievance—the grievance of sex. She was pretty and soft, and had been chivalrously treated all her days. But the present treatment by her husband and brother was everything save chivalrous. It was her custom to be helpless. They complained. Upon which impeachment of what to her was her most essential sex-prerogative, she made their lives unendurable. She no longer considered the dogs, and because she was sore and tired, she persisted in riding on the sled. She was pretty and soft, but she weighed one hundred and twenty pounds—a lusty last straw to the load dragged by the weak and starving animals. She rode for days, till they fell in the traces and the sled stood still. Charles and Hal begged her to get off and walk, pleaded with her, entreated, the while she wept and importuned Heaven with a recital of their brutality.

On one occasion they took her off the sled by main strength. They never did it again. She let her legs go limp like a spoiled child, and sat down on the trail. They went on their way, but she did not move. After they had travelled three miles they unloaded the sled, came back for her, and by main strength put her on the sled again.

In the excess of their own misery they were callous to the suffering of their animals. Hal's theory, which he practised on others, was that one must get hardened. He had started out preaching it to his sister and brother-in-law. Failing there, he hammered it into the dogs with a club. At the Five Fingers the dog-food gave out, and a toothless old squaw offered to trade them a few pounds of frozen horse-hide for the Colt's revolver that kept the big hunting-knife company at Hal's hip. A poor substitute for food was this hide, just as it had been stripped from the starved horses of the cattlemen six months back. In its frozen state it was more like strips of galvanized iron, and when a dog wrestled it into his stomach it thawed into thin and innutritious leathery strings and into a mass of short hair, irritating and indigestible.

And through it all Buck staggered along at the head of the team as in a nightmare. He pulled when he could; when he could no longer pull, he fell down and remained down till blows from whip or club drove him to his feet again. All the stiffness and gloss had gone out of his beautiful furry coat. The hair hung down, limp and draggled, or matted with dried blood where Hal's club had bruised him. His muscles had wasted away to knotty strings, and the flesh pads had disappeared, so that each rib and every bone in his frame were outlined cleanly through the loose hide that was wrinkled in folds of emptiness. It was heartbreaking, only Buck's heart was unbreakable. The man in the red sweater had proved that.

As it was with Buck, so was it with his mates. They were perambulating skeletons. There were seven all together, incuding him. In their very great misery they had become insensible to the bite of the lash or the bruise of the club. The pain of the beating was dull and distant, just as the things their eyes saw and their ears heard seemed dull and distant. They were not half living, or quarter living. They were simply so many bags of bones in which sparks of life fluttered faintly. When a halt was made, they dropped down in the traces like dead dogs, and the spark dimmed and paled and seemed to go out. And when the club or whip fell upon them, the spark fluttered feebly up, and they tottered to their feet and staggered on.

There came a day when Billee, the good-natured, fell and could not rise. Hal had traded off his revolver, so he took the axe and knocked Billee on the head as he lay in the traces, then cut the carcass out of the harness and dragged it to one side. Buck saw, and his mates saw, and they knew that this thing was very close to them. On the next day Koona went, and but five of them remained: Joe, too far gone to be malignant; Pike, crippled and limping, only half conscious and not conscious enough longer to malinger; Sol-leks, the one-eyed, still faithful to the toil of trace and trail, and mournful in that he had so little strength with which to pull; Teek, who had not travelled so far that winter and who was now beaten more than the others because he was fresher; and Buck, still at the head of the team, but no longer enforcing discipline or striving to enforce it, blind with weakness half the time and keeping the trail by the loom of it and by the dim feel of his feet.

It was beautiful spring weather, but neither dogs nor humans were aware of it. Each day the sun rose earlier and set later. It was dawn by three in the morning, and twilight lingered till nine at night. The whole long day was a blaze of sunshine. The ghostly winter silence had given way to the great spring murmur of awakening life. This murmur arose from all the land, fraught with the joy of living. It came from the things that lived and moved again, things which had been as dead and which had not moved during the long months of frost. The sap was rising in the pines. The willows and aspens were bursting out in young buds. Shrubs and vines were putting on fresh garbs of green. Crickets sang in the nights, and in the days all manner of creeping, crawling things rustled forth into the sun. Partridges and woodpeckers were booming and knocking in the forest. Squirrels were chattering, birds singing, and overhead honked the wild-fowl driving up from the south in cunning wedges that split the air.

From every hill slope came the trickle of running water, the music of unseen fountains. All things were thawing, bending, snapping. The Yukon was straining to break loose the ice that bound it down. It ate away from beneath; the sun ate from above. Air-holes formed, fissures sprang and spread apart, while thin sections of ice fell through bodily into the river. And amid all this bursting, rending, throbbing of awakening life, under the blazing sun and through the soft-sighing breezes, like wayfarers to death, staggered the two men, the woman, and the huskies.

1365   With the dogs falling, Mercedes weeping and riding, Hal swearing innocuously, and Charles's eyes wistfully watering, they staggered into John Thornton's camp at the mouth of White River. When they halted, the dogs dropped down as though they had all been struck dead. Mercedes dried her eyes and looked at John Thornton. Charles sat down on a log to rest. He sat down very slowly and painstakingly what of his great

1370 stiffness. Hal did the talking. John Thornton was whittling the last touches on an axe-handle he had made from a stick of birch. He whittled and listened, gave monosyllabic replies, and, when it was asked, terse advice. He knew the breed, and he gave his advice in the certainty that it would not be followed.

    "They told us up above that the bottom was dropping out of the trail and that the

1375 best thing for us to do was to lay over," Hal said in response to Thornton's warning to take no more chances on the rotten ice. "They told us we couldn't make White River, and here we are." This last with a sneering ring of triumph in it.

    "And they told you true," John Thornton answered. "The bottom's likely to drop out at any moment. Only fools, with the blind luck of fools, could have made it. I tell

1380 you straight, I wouldn't risk my carcass on that ice for all the gold in Alaska."

    "That's because you're not a fool, I suppose," said Hal. "All the same, we'll go on to Dawson." He uncoiled his whip. "Get up there, Buck! Hi! Get up there! Mush on!"

    Thornton went on whittling. It was idle, he knew, to get between a fool and his folly; while two or three fools more or less would not alter the scheme of things.

1385   But the team did not get up at the command. It had long since passed into the stage where blows were required to rouse it. The whip flashed out, here and there, on its merciless errands. John Thornton compressed his lips. Sol-leks was the first to crawl to his feet. Teek followed. Joe came next, yelping with pain. Pike made painful efforts. Twice he fell over, when half up, and on the third attempt managed to rise. Buck made

1390 no effort. He lay quietly where he had fallen. The lash bit into him again and again, but he neither whined nor struggled. Several times Thornton started, as though to speak, but changed his mind. A moisture came into his eyes, and, as the whipping continued, he arose and walked irresolutely up and down.

    This was the first time Buck had failed, in itself a sufficient reason to drive Hal

1395 into a rage. He exchanged the whip for the customary club. Buck refused to move under the rain of heavier blows which now fell upon him. Like his mates, he was barely able to get up, but, unlike them, he had made up his mind not to get up. He had a vague feeling of impending doom. This had been strong upon him when he pulled in to the bank, and it had not departed from him. What of the thin and rotten ice he had felt under his feet all day, it seemed that he sensed disaster close at hand, out there ahead on the ice where his master was trying to drive him. He refused to stir. So greatly had he suffered, and so far gone was he, that the blows did not hurt much. And as they continued to fall upon him, the spark of life within flickered and went down. It was nearly out. He felt strangely numb. As though from a great distance, he was aware that he was being beaten. The last sensations of pain left him. He no longer felt anything, though very faintly he could hear the impact of the club upon his body. But it was no longer his body, it seemed so far away.

And then, suddenly, without warning, uttering a cry that was inarticulate and more like the cry of an animal, John Thornton sprang upon the man who wielded the club. Hal was hurled backward, as though struck by a falling tree. Mercedes screamed. Charles looked on wistfully, wiped his watery eyes, but did not get up because of his stiffness.

John Thornton stood over Buck, struggling to control himself, too convulsed with rage to speak.

"If you strike that dog again, I'll kill you," he at last managed to say in a choking voice.

"It's my dog," Hal replied, wiping the blood from his mouth as he came back. "Get out of my way, or I'll fix you. I'm going to Dawson."

Thornton stood between him and Buck, and evinced no intention of getting out of the way. Hal drew his long hunting-knife. Mercedes screamed, cried, laughed, and manifested the chaotic abandonment of hysteria. Thornton rapped Hal's knuckles with the axe-handle, knocking the knife to the ground. He rapped his knuckles again as he tried to pick it up. Then he stooped, picked it up himself, and with two strokes cut Buck's traces.

Hal had no fight left in him. Besides, his hands were full with his sister, or his arms, rather; while Buck was too near dead to be of further use in hauling the sled. A few minutes later they pulled out from the bank and down the river. Buck heard them go and raised his head to see. Pike was leading, Sol-leks was at the wheel, and between were Joe and Teek. They were limping and staggering. Mercedes was riding the loaded sled. Hal guided at the gee-pole, and Charles stumbled along in the rear.

As Buck watched them, Thornton knelt beside him and with rough, kindly hands searched for broken bones. By the time his search had disclosed nothing more than many bruises and a state of terrible starvation, the sled was a quarter of a mile away. Dog and man watched it crawling along over the ice. Suddenly, they saw its back end drop down, as into a rut, and the gee-pole, with Hal clinging to it, jerk into the air. Mercedes's scream came to their ears. They saw Charles turn and make one step to run back, and then a whole section of ice give way and dogs and humans disappear. A yawning hole was all that was to be seen. The bottom had dropped out of the trail.

John Thornton and Buck looked at each other.

"You poor devil," said John Thornton, and Buck licked his hand.

CHAPTER SIX

For the Love of a Man

WHEN JOHN THORNTON froze his feet in the previous December, his partners had made him comfortable and left him to get well, going on themselves up the river to get out a raft of saw-logs for Dawson. He was still limping slightly at the time he rescued Buck, but with the continued warm weather even the slight limp left him. And here, **1445** lying by the river bank through the long spring days, watching the running water, listening lazily to the songs of birds and the hum of nature, Buck slowly won back his strength.

A rest comes very good after one has travelled three thousand miles, and it must be confessed that Buck waxed lazy as his wounds healed, his muscles swelled out, and the flesh came back to cover his bones. For that matter, they were all loafing,—Buck, John **1450** Thornton, and Skeet and Nig,—waiting for the raft to come that was to carry them down to Dawson. Skeet was a little Irish setter who early made friends with Buck, who, in a dying condition, was unable to resent her first advances. She had the doctor trait which some dogs possess; and as a mother cat washes her kittens, so she washed and cleansed Buck's wounds. Regularly, each morning after he had finished his breakfast, she **1455** performed her self-appointed task, till he came to look for her ministrations as much as he did for Thornton's. Nig, equally friendly, though less demonstrative, was a huge black dog, half bloodhound and half deerhound, with eyes that laughed and a boundless good nature.

To Buck's surprise these dogs manifested no jealousy toward him. They seemed

1460 to share the kindliness and largeness of John Thornton. As Buck grew stronger they enticed him into all sorts of ridiculous games, in which Thornton himself could not forbear to join; and in this fashion Buck romped through his convalescence and into a new existence. Love, genuine passionate love, was his for the first time. This he had never experienced at Judge Miller's down in the sun-kissed Santa Clara Valley. With the 1465 Judge's sons, hunting and tramping, it had been a working partnership; with the Judge's grandsons, a sort of pompous guardianship; and with the Judge himself, a stately and dignified friendship. But love that was feverish and burning, that was adoration, that was madness, it had taken John Thornton to arouse.

This man had saved his life, which was something; but, further, he was the ideal 1470 master. Other men saw to the welfare of their dogs from a sense of duty and business expediency; he saw to the welfare of his as if they were his own children, because he could not help it. And he saw further. He never forgot a kindly greeting or a cheering word, and to sit down for a long talk with them ("gas" he called it) was as much his delight as theirs. He had a way of taking Buck's head roughly between his hands, and 1475 resting his own head upon Buck's, of shaking him back and forth, the while calling him ill names that to Buck were love names. Buck knew no greater joy than that rough embrace and the sound of murmured oaths, and at each jerk back and forth it seemed that his heart would be shaken out of his body so great was its ecstasy. And when, released, he sprang to his feet, his mouth laughing, his eyes eloquent, his throat vibrant 1480 with unuttered sound, and in that fashion remained without movement, John Thornton would reverently exclaim, "God! you can all but speak!"

Buck had a trick of love expression that was akin to hurt. He would often seize Thornton's hand in his mouth and close so fiercely that the flesh bore the impress of his teeth for some time afterward. And as Buck understood the oaths to be love words, so 1485 the man understood this feigned bite for a caress.

For the most part, however, Buck's love was expressed in adoration. While he went wild with happiness when Thornton touched him or spoke to him, he did not seek these tokens. Unlike Skeet, who was wont to shove her nose under Thornton's hand and nudge and nudge till petted, or Nig, who would stalk up and rest his great head on 1490 Thornton's knee, Buck was content to adore at a distance. He would lie by the hour, eager, alert, at Thornton's feet, looking up into his face, dwelling upon it, studying it, following with keenest interest each fleeting expression, every movement or change of feature. Or, as chance might have it, he would lie farther away, to the side or rear, watching the outlines of the man and the occasional movements of his body. And often,

1495   such was the communion in which they lived, the strength of Buck's gaze would draw John Thornton's head around, and he would return the gaze, without speech, his heart shining out of his eyes as Buck's heart shone out.

For a long time after his rescue, Buck did not like Thornton to get out of his sight. From the moment he left the tent to when he entered it again, Buck would follow at his 1500 heels. His transient masters since he had come into the Northland had bred in him a fear that no master could be permanent. He was afraid that Thornton would pass out of his life as Perrault and François and the Scotch half-breed had passed out. Even in the night, in his dreams, he was haunted by this fear. At such times he would shake off sleep and creep through the chill to the flap of the tent, where he would stand and listen to the 1505 sound of his master's breathing.

But in spite of this great love he bore John Thornton, which seemed to bespeak the soft civilizing influence, the strain of the primitive, which the Northland had aroused in him, remained alive and active. Faithfulness and devotion, things born of fire and roof, were his; yet he retained his wildness and wiliness. He was a thing of the wild, 1510 come in from the wild to sit by John Thornton's fire, rather than a dog of the soft Southland stamped with the marks of generations of civilization. Because of his very great love, he could not steal from this man, but from any other man, in any other camp, he did not hesitate an instant; while the cunning with which he stole enabled him to escape detection.

1515   His face and body were scored by the teeth of many dogs, and he fought as fiercely as ever and more shrewdly. Skeet and Nig were too good-natured for quarrelling,—besides, they belonged to John Thornton; but the strange dog, no matter what the breed or valor, swiftly acknowledged Buck's supremacy or found himself struggling for life with a terrible antagonist. And Buck was merciless. He had learned 1520 well the law of club and fang, and he never forewent an advantage or drew back from a foe he had started on the way to Death. He had lessoned from Spitz, and from the chief fighting dogs of the police and mail, and knew there was no middle course. He must master or be mastered; while to show mercy was a weakness. Mercy did not exist in the primordial life. It was misunderstood for fear, and such misunderstandings made for 1525 death. Kill or be killed, eat or be eaten, was the law; and this mandate, down out of the depths of Time, he obeyed.

He was older than the days he had seen and the breaths he had drawn. He linked the past with the present, and the eternity behind him throbbed through him in a mighty rhythm to which he swayed as the tides and seasons swayed. He sat by John Thornton's

1530 fire, a broad-breasted dog, white-fanged and long-furred; but behind him were the shades of all manner of dogs, half-wolves and wild wolves, urgent and prompting, tasting the savor of the meat he ate, thirsting for the water he drank, scenting the wind with him, listening with him and telling him the sounds made by the wild life in the forest, dictating his moods, directing his actions, lying down to sleep with him when he lay down, and 1535 dreaming with him and beyond him and becoming themselves the stuff of his dreams.

So peremptorily did these shades beckon him, that each day mankind and the claims of mankind slipped farther from him. Deep in the forest a call was sounding, and as often as he heard this call, mysteriously thrilling and luring, he felt compelled to turn his back upon the fire and the beaten earth around it, and to plunge into the forest, and 1540 on and on, he knew not where or why; nor did he wonder where or why, the call sounding imperiously, deep in the forest. But as often as he gained the soft unbroken earth and the green shade, the love for John Thornton drew him back to the fire again.

Thornton alone held him. The rest of mankind was as nothing. Chance travellers might praise or pet him; but he was cold under it all, and from a too demonstrative man 1545 he would get up and walk away. When Thornton's partners, Hans and Pete, arrived on the long-expected raft, Buck refused to notice them till he learned they were close to Thornton; after that he tolerated them in a passive sort of way, accepting favors from them as though he favored them by accepting. They were of the same large type as Thornton, living close to the earth, thinking simply and seeing clearly; and ere they swung 1550 the raft into the big eddy by the saw-mill at Dawson, they understood Buck and his ways, and did not insist upon an intimacy such as obtained with Skeet and Nig.

For Thornton, however, his love seemed to grow and grow. He, alone among men, could put a pack upon Buck's back in the summer travelling. Nothing was too great for Buck to do, when Thornton commanded. One day (they had grub-staked 1555 themselves from the proceeds of the raft and left Dawson for the head-waters of the Tanana) the men and dogs were sitting on the crest of a cliff which fell away, straight down, to naked bed-rock three hundred feet below. John Thornton was sitting near the edge, Buck at his shoulder. A thoughtless whim seized Thornton, and he drew the attention of Hans and Pete to the experiment he had in mind. "Jump, Buck!" he 1560 commanded, sweeping his arm out and over the chasm. The next instant he was grappling with Buck on the extreme edge, while Hans and Pete were dragging them back into safety.

"It's uncanny," Pete said, after it was over and they had caught their speech.

Thornton shook his head. "No, it is splendid, and it is terrible, too. Do you know, it sometimes makes me afraid."

"I'm not hankering to be the man that lays hands on you while he's around," Pete announced conclusively, nodding his head toward Buck.

"Py Jingo!" was Hans's contribution. "Not mineself either."

It was at Circle City, ere the year was out, that Pete's apprehensions were realized. "Black" Burton, a man evil-tempered and malicious, had been picking a quarrel with a tenderfoot at the bar, when Thornton stepped good-naturedly between. Buck, as was his custom, was lying in a corner, head on paws, watching his master's every action. Burton struck out, without warning, straight from the shoulder. Thornton was sent spinning, and saved himself from falling only by clutching the rail of the bar.

Those who were looking on heard what was neither bark nor yelp, but a something which is best described as a roar, and they saw Buck's body rise up in the air as he left the floor for Burton's throat. The man saved his life by instinctively throwing out his arm, but was hurled backward to the floor with Buck on top of him. Buck loosed his teeth from the flesh of the arm and drove in again for the throat. This time the man succeeded only in partly blocking, and his throat was torn open. Then the crowd was upon Buck, and he was driven off; but while a surgeon checked the bleeding, he prowled up and down, growling furiously, attempting to rush in, and being forced back by an array of hostile clubs. A "miners' meeting," called on the spot, decided that the dog had sufficient provocation, and Buck was discharged. But his reputation was made, and from that day his name spread through every camp in Alaska.

Later on, in the fall of the year, he saved John Thornton's life in quite another fashion. The three partners were lining a long and narrow poling-boat down a bad stretch of rapids on the Forty-Mile Creek. Hans and Pete moved along the bank, snubbing with a thin Manila rope from tree to tree, while Thornton remained in the boat, helping its descent by means of a pole, and shouting directions to the shore. Buck, on the bank, worried and anxious, kept abreast of the boat, his eyes never off his master.

At a particularly bad spot, where a ledge of barely submerged rocks jutted out into the river, Hans cast off the rope, and, while Thornton poled the boat out into the stream, ran down the bank with the end in his hand to snub the boat when it had cleared the ledge. This it did, and was flying down-stream in a current as swift as a mill-race, when Hans checked it with the rope and checked too suddenly. The boat flirted over and snubbed in to the bank bottom up, while Thornton, flung sheer out of it, was carried down-stream toward the worst part of the rapids, a stretch of wild water in which no swimmer could live.

1600 Buck had sprung in on the instant; and at the end of three hundred yards, amid a mad swirl of water, he overhauled Thornton. When he felt him grasp his tail, Buck headed for the bank, swimming with all his splendid strength. But the progress shoreward was slow; the progress down-stream amazingly rapid. From below came the fatal roaring where the wild current went wilder and was rent in shreds and spray by the

1605 rocks which thrust through like the teeth of an enormous comb. The suck of the water as it took the beginning of the last steep pitch was frightful, and Thornton knew that the shore was impossible. He scraped furiously over a rock, bruised across a second, and struck a third with crushing force. He clutched its slippery top with both hands, releasing Buck, and above the roar of the churning water shouted: "Go, Buck! Go!"

1610 Buck could not hold his own, and swept on down-stream, struggling desperately, but unable to win back. When he heard Thornton's command repeated, he partly reared out of the water, throwing his head high, as though for a last look, then turned obediently toward the bank. He swam powerfully and was dragged ashore by Pete and Hans at the very point where swimming ceased to be possible and destruction began.

1615 They knew that the time a man could cling to a slippery rock in the face of that driving current was a matter of minutes, and they ran as fast as they could up the bank to a point far above where Thornton was hanging on. They attached the line with which they had been snubbing the boat to Buck's neck and shoulders, being careful that it should neither strangle him nor impede his swimming, and launched him into the stream.

1620 He struck out boldly, but not straight enough into the stream. He discovered the mistake too late, when Thornton was abreast of him and a bare half-dozen strokes away while he was being carried helplessly past.

Hans promptly snubbed with the rope, as though Buck were a boat. The rope thus tightening on him in the sweep of the current, he was jerked under the surface, and

1625 under the surface he remained till his body struck against the bank and he was hauled out. He was half drowned, and Hans and Pete threw themselves upon him, pounding the breath into him and the water out of him. He staggered to his feet and fell down. The faint sound of Thornton's voice came to them, and though they could not make out the words of it, they knew that he was in his extremity. His master's voice acted on Buck

1630 like an electric shock. He sprang to his feet and ran up the bank ahead of the men to the point of his previous departure.

Again the rope was attached and he was launched, and again he struck out, but this time straight into the stream. He had miscalculated once, but he would not be guilty of it a second time. Hans paid out the rope, permitting no slack, while Pete kept it clear of coils. Buck held on till he was on a line straight above Thornton; then he turned, and with the speed of an express train headed down upon him. Thornton saw him coming, and, as Buck struck him like a battering ram, with the whole force of the current behind him, he reached up and closed with both arms around the shaggy neck. Hans snubbed the rope around the tree, and Buck and Thornton were jerked under the water. Strangling, suffocating, sometimes one uppermost and sometimes the other, dragging over the jagged bottom, smashing against rocks and snags, they veered in to the bank.

Thornton came to, belly downward and being violently propelled back and forth across a drift log by Hans and Pete. His first glance was for Buck, over whose limp and apparently lifeless body Nig was setting up a howl, while Skeet was licking the wet face and closed eyes. Thornton was himself bruised and battered, and he went carefully over Buck's body, when he had been brought around, finding three broken ribs.

"That settles it," he announced. "We camp right here." And camp they did, till Buck's ribs knitted and he was able to travel.

That winter, at Dawson, Buck performed another exploit, not so heroic, perhaps, but one that put his name many notches higher on the totem-pole of Alaskan fame. This exploit was particularly gratifying to the three men; for they stood in need of the outfit which it furnished, and were enabled to make a long-desired trip into the virgin East, where miners had not yet appeared. It was brought about by a conversation in the Eldorado Saloon, in which men waxed boastful of their favorite dogs. Buck, because of his record, was the target for these men, and Thornton was driven stoutly to defend him. At the end of half an hour one man stated that his dog could start a sled with five hundred pounds and walk off with it; a second bragged six hundred for his dog; and a third, seven hundred.

"Pooh! pooh!" said John Thornton; "Buck can start a thousand pounds."

"And break it out? and walk off with it for a hundred yards?" demanded Matthewson, a Bonanza King, he of the seven hundred vaunt.

"And break it out, and walk off with it for a hundred yards," John Thornton said coolly.

"Well," Matthewson said, slowly and deliberately, so that all could hear, "I've got a thousand dollars that says he can't. And there it is." So saying, he slammed a sack of gold dust of the size of a bologna sausage down upon the bar.

Nobody spoke. Thornton's bluff, if bluff it was, had been called. He could feel a flush of warm blood creeping up his face. His tongue had tricked him. He did not know whether Buck could start a thousand pounds. Half a ton! The enormousness of it appalled him. He had great faith in Buck's strength and had often thought him capable of starting such a load; but never, as now, had he faced the possibility of it, the eyes of a dozen men fixed upon him, silent and waiting. Further, he had no thousand dollars; nor had Hans or Pete.

"I've got a sled standing outside now, with twenty fifty-pound sacks of flour on it," Matthewson went on with brutal directness; "so don't let that hinder you."

Thornton did not reply. He did not know what to say. He glanced from face to face in the absent way of a man who has lost the power of thought and is seeking somewhere to find the thing that will start it going again. The face of Jim O'Brien, a Mastodon King and old-time comrade, caught his eyes. It was as a cue to him, seeming to rouse him to do what he would never have dreamed of doing.

"Can you lend me a thousand?" he asked, almost in a whisper.

"Sure," answered O'Brien, thumping down a plethoric sack by the side of Matthewson's. "Though it's little faith I'm having, John, that the beast can do the trick."

The Eldorado emptied its occupants into the street to see the test. The tables were deserted, and the dealers and gamekeepers came forth to see the outcome of the wager and to lay odds. Several hundred men, furred and mittened, banked around the sled within easy distance. Matthewson's sled, loaded with a thousand pounds of flour, had been standing for a couple of hours, and in the intense cold (it was sixty below zero) the runners had frozen fast to the hard-packed snow. Men offered odds of two to one that Buck could not budge the sled. A quibble arose concerning the phrase "break out." O'Brien contended it was Thornton's privilege to knock the runners loose, leaving Buck to "break it out" from a dead standstill. Matthewson insisted that the phrase included breaking the runners from the frozen grip of the snow. A majority of the men who had witnessed the making of the bet decided in his favor, whereat the odds went up to three to one against Buck.

There were no takers. Not a man believed him capable of the feat. Thornton had been hurried into the wager, heavy with doubt; and now that he looked at the sled itself, the concrete fact, with the regular team of ten dogs curled up in the snow before it, the more impossible the task appeared. Matthewson waxed jubilant.

"Three to one!" he proclaimed. "I'll lay you another thousand at that figure, Thornton. What d'ye say?"

Thornton's doubt was strong in his face, but his fighting spirit was aroused—the fighting spirit that soars above odds, fails to recognize the impossible, and is deaf to all save the clamor for battle. He called Hans and Pete to him. Their sacks were slim, and with his own the three partners could rake together only two hundred dollars. In the ebb of their fortunes, this sum was their total capital; yet they laid it unhesitatingly against Matthewson's six hundred.

The team of ten dogs was unhitched, and Buck, with his own harness, was put into the sled. He had caught the contagion of the excitement, and he felt that in some way he must do a great thing for John Thornton. Murmurs of admiration at his splendid appearance went up. He was in perfect condition, without an ounce of superfluous flesh, and the one hundred and fifty pounds that he weighed were so many pounds of grit and virility. His furry coat shone with the sheen of silk. Down the neck and across the shoulders, his mane, in repose as it was, half bristled and seemed to lift with every movement, as though excess of vigor made each particular hair alive and active. The great breast and heavy fore legs were no more than in proportion with the rest of the body, where the muscles showed in tight rolls underneath the skin. Men felt these muscles and proclaimed them hard as iron, and the odds went down to two to one.

"Gad, sir! Gad, sir!" stuttered a member of the latest dynasty, a king of the Skookum Benches. "I offer you eight hundred for him, sir, before the test, sir; eight hundred just as he stands."

Thornton shook his head and stepped to Buck's side.

"You must stand off from him," Matthewson protested. "Free play and plenty of room."

The crowd fell silent; only could be heard the voices of the gamblers vainly offering two to one. Everybody acknowledged Buck a magnificent animal, but twenty fifty-pound sacks of flour bulked too large in their eyes for them to loosen their pouch-strings.

Thornton knelt down by Buck's side. He took his head in his two hands and rested cheek on cheek. He did not playfully shake him, as was his wont, or murmur soft love curses; but he whispered in his ear. "As you love me, Buck. As you love me," was what he whispered. Buck whined with suppressed eagerness.

The crowd was watching curiously. The affair was growing mysterious. It seemed like a conjuration. As Thornton got to his feet, Buck seized his mittened hand between his jaws, pressing in with his teeth and releasing slowly, half-reluctantly. It was the answer, in terms, not of speech, but of love. Thornton stepped well back.

"Now, Buck," he said.

Buck tightened the traces, then slacked them for a matter of several inches. It was the way he had learned.

1740 "Gee!" Thornton's voice rang out, sharp in the tense silence.

Buck swung to the right, ending the movement in a plunge that took up the slack and with a sudden jerk arrested his one hundred and fifty pounds. The load quivered, and from under the runners arose a crisp crackling.

"Haw!" Thornton commanded.

1745 Buck duplicated the manœuvre, this time to the left. The crackling turned into a snapping, the sled pivoting and the runners slipping and grating several inches to the side. The sled was broken out. Men were holding their breaths, intensely unconscious of the fact.

"Now, MUSH!"

1750 Thornton's command cracked out like a pistol-shot. Buck threw himself forward, tightening the traces with a jarring lunge. His whole body was gathered compactly together in the tremendous effort, the muscles writhing and knotting like live things under the silky fur. His great chest was low to the ground, his head forward and down, while his feet were flying like mad, the claws scarring the hard-packed snow in parallel
1755 grooves. The sled swayed and trembled, half-started forward. One of his feet slipped, and one man groaned aloud. Then the sled lurched ahead in what appeared a rapid succession of jerks, though it never really came to a dead stop again . . . half an inch . . . an inch . . . two inches. . . . The jerks perceptibly diminished; as the sled gained momentum, he caught them up, till it was moving steadily along.

1760 Men gasped and began to breathe again, unaware that for a moment they had ceased to breathe. Thornton was running behind, encouraging Buck with short, cheery words. The distance had been measured off, and as he neared the pile of firewood which marked the end of the hundred yards, a cheer began to grow and grow, which burst into a roar as he passed the firewood and halted at command. Every man was
1765 tearing himself loose, even Matthewson. Hats and mittens were flying in the air. Men were shaking hands, it did not matter with whom, and bubbling over in a general incoherent babel.

But Thornton fell on his knees beside Buck. Head was against head, and he was shaking him back and forth. Those who hurried up heard him cursing Buck, and he
1770 cursed him long and fervently, and softly and lovingly.

"Gad, sir! Gad, sir!" spluttered the Skookum Bench king. "I'll give you a thousand for him, sir, a thousand, sir—twelve hundred, sir."

Thornton rose to his feet. His eyes were wet. The tears were streaming frankly down his cheeks. "Sir," he said to the Skookum Bench king, "no, sir. You can go to hell, sir. It's the best I can do for you, sir."

1775

Buck seized Thornton's hand in his teeth. Thornton shook him back and forth. As though animated by a common impulse, the onlookers drew back to a respectful distance; nor were they again indiscreet enough to interrupt.

CHAPTER SEVEN

The Sounding of the Call

WHEN BUCK EARNED sixteen hundred dollars in five minutes for John Thornton, he
1780   made it possible for his master to pay off certain debts and to journey with his partners
into the East after a fabled lost mine, the history of which was as old as the history of the
country. Many men had sought it; few had found it; and more than a few there were
who had never returned from the quest. This lost mine was steeped in tragedy and
shrouded in mystery. No one knew of the first man. The oldest tradition stopped before
1785   it got back to him. From the beginning there had been an ancient and ramshackle cabin.
Dying men had sworn to it, and to the mine the site of which it marked, clinching their
testimony with nuggets that were unlike any known grade of gold in the Northland.

    But no living man had looted this treasure house, and the dead were dead;
wherefore John Thornton and Pete and Hans, with Buck and half a dozen other dogs,
1790   faced into the East on an unknown trail to achieve where men and dogs as good as
themselves had failed. They sledded seventy miles up the Yukon, swung to the left into
the Stewart River, passed the Mayo and the McQuestion, and held on until the Stewart
itself became a streamlet, threading the upstanding peaks which marked the backbone of
the continent.

1795   John Thornton asked little of man or nature. He was unafraid of the wild. With
a handful of salt and a rifle he could plunge into the wilderness and fare wherever he
pleased and as long as he pleased. Being in no haste, Indian fashion, he hunted his

dinner in the course of the day's travel; and if he failed to find it, like the Indian, he kept on travelling, secure in the knowledge that sooner or later he would come to it. So, on this great journey into the East, straight meat was the bill of fare, ammunition and tools principally made up the load on the sled, and the time-card was drawn upon the limitless future.

To Buck it was boundless delight, this hunting, fishing, and indefinite wandering through strange places. For weeks at a time they would hold on steadily, day after day; and for weeks upon end they would camp, here and there, the dogs loafing and the men burning holes through frozen muck and gravel and washing countless pans of dirt by the heat of the fire. Sometimes they went hungry, sometimes they feasted riotously, all according to the abundance of game and the fortune of hunting. Summer arrived, and dogs and men packed on their backs, rafted across blue mountain lakes, and descended or ascended unknown rivers in slender boats whipsawed from the standing forest.

The months came and went, and back and forth they twisted through the uncharted vastness, where no men were and yet where men had been if the Lost Cabin were true. They went across divides in summer blizzards, shivered under the midnight sun on naked mountains between the timber line and the eternal snows, dropped into summer valleys amid swarming gnats and flies, and in the shadows of glaciers picked strawberries and flowers as ripe and fair as any the Southland could boast. In the fall of the year they penetrated a weird lake country, sad and silent, where wild-fowl had been, but where then there was no life nor sign of life—only the blowing of chill winds, the forming of ice in sheltered places, and the melancholy rippling of waves on lonely beaches.

And through another winter they wandered on the obliterated trails of men who had gone before. Once, they came upon a path blazed through the forest, an ancient path, and the Lost Cabin seemed very near. But the path began nowhere and ended nowhere, and it remained mystery, as the man who made it and the reason he made it remained mystery. Another time they chanced upon the time-graven wreckage of a hunting lodge, and amid the shreds of rotted blankets John Thornton found a long-barrelled flint-lock. He knew it for a Hudson Bay Company gun of the young days in the Northwest, when such a gun was worth its height in beaver skins packed flat. And that was all—no hint as to the man who in an early day had reared the lodge and left the gun among the blankets.

Spring came on once more, and at the end of all their wandering they found, not the Lost Cabin, but a shallow placer in a broad valley where the gold showed like yellow butter across the bottom of the washing-pan. They sought no farther. Each day they worked earned them thousands of dollars in clean dust and nuggets, and they worked every day. The gold was sacked in moose-hide bags, fifty pounds to the bag, and piled like so much firewood outside the spruce-bough lodge. Like giants they toiled, days flashing on the heels of days like dreams as they heaped the treasure up.

There was nothing for the dogs to do, save the hauling in of meat now and again that Thornton killed, and Buck spent long hours musing by the fire. The vision of the short-legged hairy man came to him more frequently, now that there was little work to be done; and often, blinking by the fire, Buck wandered with him in that other world which he remembered.

The salient thing of this other world seemed fear. When he watched the hairy man sleeping by the fire, head between his knees and hands clasped above, Buck saw that he slept restlessly, with many starts and awakenings, at which times he would peer fearfully into the darkness and fling more wood upon the fire. Did they walk by the beach of a sea, where the hairy man gathered shell-fish and ate them as he gathered, it was with eyes that roved everywhere for hidden danger and with legs prepared to run like the wind at its first appearance. Through the forest they crept noiselessly, Buck at the hairy man's heels; and they were alert and vigilant, the pair of them, ears twitching and moving and nostrils quivering, for the man heard and smelled as keenly as Buck. The hairy man could spring up into the trees and travel ahead as fast as on the ground, swinging by the arms from limb to limb, sometimes a dozen feet apart, letting go and catching, never falling, never missing his grip. In fact, he seemed as much at home among the trees as on the ground; and Buck had memories of nights of vigil spent beneath trees wherein the hairy man roosted, holding on tightly as he slept.

And closely akin to the visions of the hairy man was the call still sounding in the depths of the forest. It filled him with a great unrest and strange desires. It caused him to feel a vague, sweet gladness, and he was aware of wild yearnings and stirrings for he knew not what. Sometimes he pursued the call into the forest, looking for it as though it were a tangible thing, barking softly or defiantly, as the mood might dictate. He would thrust his nose into the cool wood moss, or into the black soil where long grasses grew, and snort with joy at the fat earth smells; or he would crouch for hours, as if in concealment, behind fungus-covered trunks of fallen trees, wide-eyed and wide-eared to all that moved and sounded about him. It might be, lying thus, that he hoped to surprise this call he could not understand. But he did not know why he did these various things.

He was impelled to do them, and did not reason about them at all.

Irresistible impulses seized him. He would be lying in camp, dozing lazily in the heat of the day, when suddenly his head would lift and his ears cock up, intent and listening, and he would spring to his feet and dash away, and on and on, for hours, through the forest aisles and across the open spaces where the niggerheads bunched. He loved to run down dry watercourses, and to creep and spy upon the bird life in the woods. For a day at a time he would lie in the underbrush where he could watch the partridges drumming and strutting up and down. But especially he loved to run in the dim twilight of the summer midnights, listening to the subdued and sleepy murmurs of the forest, reading signs and sounds as man may read a book, and seeking for the mysterious something that called—called, waking or sleeping, at all times, for him to come.

One night he sprang from sleep with a start, eager-eyed, nostrils quivering and scenting, his mane bristling in recurrent waves. From the forest came the call (or one note of it, for the call was many noted), distinct and definite as never before,—a long-drawn howl, like, yet unlike, any noise made by husky dog. And he knew it, in the old familiar way, as a sound heard before. He sprang through the sleeping camp and in swift silence dashed through the woods. As he drew closer to the cry he went more slowly, with caution in every movement, till he came to an open place among the trees, and looking out saw, erect on haunches, with nose pointed to the sky, a long, lean, timber wolf.

He had made no noise, yet it ceased from its howling and tried to sense his presence. Buck stalked into the open, half crouching, body gathered compactly together, tail straight and stiff, feet falling with unwonted care. Every movement advertised commingled threatening and overture of friendliness. It was the menacing truce that marks the meeting of wild beasts that prey. But the wolf fled at sight of him. He followed, with wild leapings, in a frenzy to overtake. He ran him into a blind channel, in the bed of the creek, where a timber jam barred the way. The wolf whirled about, pivoting on his hind legs after the fashion of Joe and of all cornered husky dogs, snarling and bristling, clipping his teeth together in a continuous and rapid succession of snaps.

Buck did not attack, but circled him about and hedged him in with friendly advances. The wolf was suspicious and afraid; for Buck made three of him in weight, while his head barely reached Buck's shoulder. Watching his chance, he darted away, and the chase was resumed. Time and again he was cornered, and the thing repeated, though he was in poor condition, or Buck could not so easily have overtaken him. He would run till Buck's head was even with his flank, when he would whirl around at bay, only to dash away again at the first opportunity.

But in the end Buck's pertinacity was rewarded; for the wolf, finding that no harm was intended, finally sniffed noses with him. Then they became friendly, and played about in the nervous, half-coy way with which fierce beasts belie their fierceness. After some time of this the wolf started off at an easy lope in a manner that plainly showed he was going somewhere. He made it clear to Buck that he was to come, and they ran side by side through the sombre twilight, straight up the creek bed, into the gorge from which it issued, and across the bleak divide where it took its rise.

On the opposite slope of the watershed they came down into a level country where were great stretches of forest and many streams, and through these great stretches they ran steadily, hour after hour, the sun rising higher and the day growing warmer. Buck was wildly glad. He knew he was at last answering the call, running by the side of his wood brother toward the place from where the call surely came. Old memories were coming upon him fast, and he was stirring to them as of old he stirred to the realities of which they were the shadows. He had done this thing before, somewhere in that other and dimly remembered world, and he was doing it again, now, running free in the open, the unpacked earth underfoot, the wide sky overhead.

They stopped by a running stream to drink, and, stopping, Buck remembered John Thornton. He sat down. The wolf started on toward the place from where the call surely came, then returned to him, sniffing noses and making actions as though to encourage him. But Buck turned about and started slowly on the back track. For the better part of an hour the wild brother ran by his side, whining softly. Then he sat down, pointed his nose upward, and howled. It was a mournful howl, and as Buck held steadily on his way he heard it grow faint and fainter until it was lost in the distance.

John Thornton was eating dinner when Buck dashed into camp and sprang upon him in a frenzy of affection, overturning him, scrambling upon him, licking his face, biting his hand—"playing the general tom-fool," as John Thornton characterized it, the while he shook Buck back and forth and cursed him lovingly.

For two days and nights Buck never left camp, never let Thornton out of his sight. He followed him about at his work, watched him while he ate, saw him into his blankets at night and out of them in the morning. But after two days the call in the forest began to sound more imperiously than ever. Buck's restlessness came back on him, and he was haunted by recollections of the wild brother, and of the smiling land beyond the divide and the run side by side through the wide forest stretches. Once again he took to wandering in the woods, but the wild brother came no more; and though he listened through long vigils, the mournful howl was never raised.

He began to sleep out at night, staying away from the camp for days at a time; and once he crossed the divide at the head of the creek and went down into the land of timber and streams. There he wandered for a week, seeking vainly for fresh sign of the wild brother, killing his meat as he travelled and travelling with the long, easy lope that seems never to tire. He fished for salmon in a broad stream that emptied somewhere into the sea, and by this stream he killed a large black bear, blinded by the mosquitoes while likewise fishing, and raging through the forest helpless and terrible. Even so, it was a hard fight, and it aroused the last latent remnants of Buck's ferocity. And two days later, when he returned to his kill and found a dozen wolverines quarrelling over the spoil, he scattered them like chaff; and those that fled left two behind who would quarrel no more.

The blood-longing became stronger than ever before. He was a killer, a thing that preyed, living on the things that lived, unaided, alone, by virtue of his own strength and prowess, surviving triumphantly in a hostile environment where only the strong survived. Because of all this he became possessed of a great pride in himself, which communicated itself like a contagion to his physical being. It advertised itself in all his movements, was apparent in the play of every muscle, spoke plainly as speech in the way he carried himself, and made his glorious furry coat if anything more glorious. But for the stray brown on his muzzle and above his eyes, and for the splash of white hair that ran midmost down his chest, he might well have been mistaken for a gigantic wolf, larger than the largest of the breed. From his St. Bernard father he had inherited size and weight, but it was his shepherd mother who had given shape to that size and weight. His muzzle was the long wolf muzzle, save that it was larger than the muzzle of any wolf; and his head, somewhat broader, was the wolf head on a massive scale.

His cunning was wolf cunning, and wild cunning; his intelligence, shepherd intelligence and St. Bernard intelligence; and all this, plus an experience gained in the fiercest of schools, made him as formidable a creature as any that roamed the wild. A carnivorous animal, living on a straight meat diet, he was in full flower, at the high tide of his life, overspilling with vigor and virility. When Thornton passed a caressing hand along his back, a snapping and crackling followed the hand, each hair discharging its pent magnetism at the contact. Every part, brain and body, nerve tissue and fibre, was keyed to the most exquisite pitch; and between all the parts there was a perfect equilibrium or adjustment. To sights and sounds and events which required action, he responded with lightning-like rapidity. Quickly as a husky dog could leap to defend from attack or to attack, he could leap twice as quickly. He saw the movement, or heard sound, and responded in less time than another dog required to compass the mere seeing or hearing.

1975 He perceived and determined and responded in the same instant. In point of fact the three actions of perceiving, determining, and responding were sequential; but so infinitesimal were the intervals of time between them that they appeared simultaneous. His muscles were surcharged with vitality, and snapped into play sharply, like steel springs. Life streamed through him in splendid flood, glad and rampant, until it seemed

1980 that it would burst him asunder in sheer ecstasy and pour forth generously over the world.

"Never was there such a dog," said John Thornton one day, as the partners watched Buck marching out of camp.

"When he was made, the mould was broke," said Pete.

1985 "Py jingo! I t'ink so mineself," Hans affirmed.

They saw him marching out of camp, but they did not see the instant and terrible transformation which took place as soon as he was within the secrecy of the forest. He no longer marched. At once he became a thing of the wild, stealing along softly, cat-footed, a passing shadow that appeared and disappeared among the shadows. He

1990 knew how to take advantage of every cover, to crawl on his belly like a snake, and like a snake to leap and strike. He could take a ptarmigan from its nest, kill a rabbit as it slept, and snap in mid air the little chipmunks fleeing a second too late for the trees. Fish, in open pools, were not too quick for him; nor were beaver, mending their dams, too wary. He killed to eat, not from wantonness; but he preferred to eat what he killed

1995 himself. So a lurking humor ran through his deeds, and it was his delight to steal upon the squirrels, and, when he all but had them, to let them go, chattering in mortal fear to the tree-tops.

As the fall of the year came on, the moose appeared in greater abundance, moving slowly down to meet the winter in the lower and less rigorous valleys. Buck had

2000 already dragged down a stray part-grown calf; but he wished strongly for larger and more formidable quarry, and he came upon it one day on the divide at the head of the creek. A band of twenty moose had crossed over from the land of streams and timber, and chief among them was a great bull. He was in a savage temper, and, standing over six feet from the ground, was as formidable an antagonist as even Buck could desire. Back and forth the bull tossed his great palmated antlers, branching to fourteen points and embracing seven feet within the tips. His small eyes burned with a vicious and bitter light, while he roared with fury at sight of Buck.

From the bull's side, just forward of the flank, protruded a feathered arrow-end, which accounted for his savageness. Guided by that instinct which came from the old hunting days of the primordial world, Buck proceeded to cut the bull out from the herd. It was no slight task. He would bark and dance about in front of the bull, just out of reach of the great antlers and of the terrible splay hoofs which could have stamped his life out with a single blow. Unable to turn his back on the fanged danger and go on, the bull would be driven into paroxysms of rage. At such moments he charged Buck, who retreated craftily, luring him on by a simulated inability to escape. But when he was thus separated from his fellows, two or three of the younger bulls would charge back upon Buck and enable the wounded bull to rejoin the herd.

There is a patience of the wild—dogged, tireless, persistent at life itself—that holds motionless for endless hours the spider in its web, the snake in its coils, the panther in its ambuscade; this patience belongs peculiarly to life when it hunts its living food; and it belonged to Buck as he clung to the flank of the herd, retarding its march, irritating the young bulls, worrying the cows with their half-grown calves, and driving the wounded bull mad with helpless rage. For half a day this continued. Buck multiplied himself, attacking from all sides, enveloping the herd in a whirlwind of menace, cutting out his victim as fast as it could rejoin its mates, wearing out the patience of creatures preyed upon, which is a lesser patience than that of creatures preying.

As the day wore along and the sun dropped to its bed in the northwest (the darkness had come back and the fall nights were six hours long), the young bulls retraced their steps more and more reluctantly to the aid of their beset leader. The down-coming winter was harrying them on to the lower levels, and it seemed they could never shake off this tireless creature that held them back. Besides, it was not the life of the herd, or of the young bulls, that was threatened. The life of only one member was demanded, which was a remoter interest than their lives, and in the end they were content to pay the toll.

As twilight fell the old bull stood with lowered head, watching his mates—the cows he had known, the calves he had fathered, the bulls he had mastered—as they shambled on at a rapid pace through the fading light. He could not follow, for before his nose leaped the merciless fanged terror that would not let him go. Three hundredweight more than half a ton he weighed; he had lived a long, strong life, full of fight and struggle, and at the end he faced death at the teeth of a creature whose head did not reach beyond his great knuckled knees.

From then on, night and day, Buck never left his prey, never gave it a moment's rest, never permitted it to browse the leaves of trees or the shoots of young birch and willow. Nor did he give the wounded bull opportunity to slake his burning thirst in the slender trickling streams they crossed. Often, in desperation, he burst into long stretches of flight. At such times Buck did not attempt to stay him, but loped easily at his heels, satisfied with the way the game was played, lying down when the moose stood still, attacking him fiercely when he strove to eat or drink.

The great head drooped more and more under its tree of horns, and the shambling trot grew weak and weaker. He took to standing for long periods, with nose to the ground and dejected ears dropped limply; and Buck found more time in which to get water for himself and in which to rest. At such moments, panting with red lolling tongue and with eyes fixed upon the big bull, it appeared to Buck that a change was coming over the face of things. He could feel a new stir in the land. As the moose were coming into the land, other kinds of life were coming in. Forest and stream and air seemed palpitant with their presence. The news of it was borne in upon him, not by sight, or sound, or smell, but by some other and subtler sense. He heard nothing, saw nothing, yet knew that the land was somehow different; that through it strange things were afoot and ranging; and he resolved to investigate after he had finished the business in hand.

At last, at the end of the fourth day, he pulled the great moose down. For a day and a night he remained by the kill, eating and sleeping, turn and turn about. Then, rested, refreshed and strong, he turned his face toward camp and John Thornton. He broke into the long easy lope, and went on, hour after hour, never at loss for the tangled way, heading straight home through strange country with a certitude of direction that put man and his magnetic needle to shame.

As he held on he became more and more conscious of the new stir in the land. There was life abroad in it different from the life which had been there throughout the summer. No longer was this fact borne in upon him in some subtle, mysterious way. The birds talked of it, the squirrels chattered about it, the very breeze whispered of it. Several times he stopped and drew in the fresh morning air in great sniffs, reading a message which made him leap on with greater speed. He was oppressed with a sense of calamity happening, if it were not calamity already happened; and as he crossed the last watershed and dropped down into the valley toward camp, he proceeded with greater caution.

Three miles away he came upon a fresh trail that sent his neck hair rippling and bristling. It led straight toward camp and John Thornton. Buck hurried on, swiftly and stealthily, every nerve straining and tense, alert to the multitudinous details which told a story—all but the end. His nose gave him a varying description of the passage of the life on the heels of which he was travelling. He remarked the pregnant silence of the forest. The bird life had flitted. The squirrels were in hiding. One only he saw,—a sleek gray fellow, flattened against a gray dead limb so that he seemed a part of it, a woody excrescence upon the wood itself.

As Buck slid along with the obscureness of a gliding shadow, his nose was jerked suddenly to the side as though a positive force had gripped and pulled it. He followed the new scent into a thicket and found Nig. He was lying on his side, dead where he had dragged himself, an arrow protruding, head and feathers, from either side of his body.

A hundred yards farther on, Buck came upon one of the sled-dogs Thornton had bought in Dawson. This dog was thrashing about in a death-struggle, directly on the trail, and Buck passed around him without stopping. From the camp came the faint sound of many voices, rising and falling in a sing-song chant. Bellying forward to the edge of the clearing, he found Hans, lying on his face, feathered with arrows like a porcupine. At the same instant Buck peered out where the spruce-bough lodge had been and saw what made his hair leap straight up on his neck and shoulders. A gust of overpowering rage swept over him. He did not know that he growled, but he growled aloud with a terrible ferocity. For the last time in his life he allowed passion to usurp cunning and reason, and it was because of his great love for John Thornton that he lost his head.

The Yeehats were dancing about the wreckage of the spruce-bough lodge when they heard a fearful roaring and saw rushing upon them an animal the like of which they had never seen before. It was Buck, a live hurricane of fury, hurling himself upon them in a frenzy to destroy. He sprang at the foremost man (it was the chief of the Yeehats), ripping the throat wide open till the rent jugular spouted a fountain of blood. He did not pause to worry the victim, but ripped in passing, with the next bound tearing wide the throat of a second man. There was no withstanding him. He plunged about in their very midst, tearing, rending, destroying, in constant and terrific motion which defied the arrows they discharged at him. In fact, so inconceivably rapid were his movements, and so closely were the Indians tangled together, that they shot one another with the arrows; and one young hunter, hurling a spear at Buck in mid air, drove it through the chest of another hunter with such force that the point broke through the skin of the back and stood out beyond. Then a panic seized the Yeehats, and they fled in terror to the woods, proclaiming as they fled the advent of the Evil Spirit.

And truly Buck was the Fiend incarnate, raging at their heels and dragging them down like deer as they raced through the trees. It was a fateful day for the Yeehats. They scattered far and wide over the country, and it was not till a week later that the last of the survivors gathered together in a lower valley and counted their losses. As for Buck, wearying of the pursuit, he returned to the desolated camp. He found Pete where he had been killed in his blankets in the first moment of surprise. Thornton's desperate struggle was fresh-written on the earth, and Buck scented every detail of it down to the edge of a deep pool. By the edge, head and fore feet in the water, lay Skeet, faithful to the last. The pool itself, muddy and discolored from the sluice boxes, effectually hid what it contained, and it contained John Thornton; for Buck followed his trace into the water, from which no trace led away.

All day Buck brooded by the pool or roamed restlessly about the camp. Death, as a cessation of movement, as a passing out and away from the lives of the living, he knew, and he knew John Thornton was dead. It left a great void in him, somewhat akin to hunger, but a void which ached and ached, and which food could not fill. At times, when he paused to contemplate the carcasses of the Yeehats, he forgot the pain of it; and at such times he was aware of a great pride in himself,—a pride greater than any he had yet experienced. He had killed man, the noblest game of all, and he had killed in the face of the law of club and fang. He sniffed the bodies curiously. They had died so easily. It was harder to kill a husky dog than them. They were no match at all, were it not for their arrows and spears and clubs. Thenceforward he would be unafraid of them except when they bore in their hands their arrows, spears, and clubs.

Night came on, and a full moon rose high over the trees into the sky, lighting the land till it lay bathed in ghostly day. And with the coming of the night, brooding and mourning by the pool, Buck became alive to a stirring of the new life in the forest other than that which the Yeehats had made. He stood up, listening and scenting. From far away drifted a faint, sharp yelp, followed by a chorus of similar sharp yelps. As the moments passed the yelps grew closer and louder. Again Buck knew them as things heard in that other world which persisted in his memory. He walked to the centre of the open space and listened. It was the call, the many-noted call, sounding more luringly and compellingly than ever before. And as never before, he was ready to obey. John Thornton was dead. The last tie was broken. Man and the claims of man no longer bound him.

2145   Hunting their living meat, as the Yeehats were hunting it, on the flanks of the migrating moose, the wolf pack had at last crossed over from the land of streams and timber and invaded Buck's valley. Into the clearing where the moonlight streamed, they poured in a silvery flood; and in the centre of the clearing stood Buck, motionless as a statue, waiting their coming. They were awed, so still and large he stood, and a

2150   moment's pause fell, till the boldest one leaped straight for him. Like a flash Buck struck, breaking the neck. Then he stood, without movement, as before, the stricken wolf rolling in agony behind him. Three others tried it in sharp succession; and one after the other they drew back, streaming blood from slashed throats or shoulders.

    This was sufficient to fling the whole pack forward, pell-mell, crowded together,

2155   blocked and confused by its eagerness to pull down the prey. Buck's marvellous quickness and agility stood him in good stead. Pivoting on his hind legs, and snapping and gashing, he was everywhere at once, presenting a front which was apparently unbroken so swiftly did he whirl and guard from side to side. But to prevent them from getting behind him, he was forced back, down past the pool and into the creek bed, till

2160   he brought up against a high gravel bank. He worked along to a right angle in the bank which the men had made in the course of mining, and in this angle he came to bay, protected on three sides and with nothing to do but face the front.

    And so well did he face it, that at the end of half an hour the wolves drew back discomfited. The tongues of all were out and lolling, the white fangs showing cruelly

2165   white in the moonlight. Some were lying down with heads raised and ears pricked forward; others stood on their feet, watching him; and still others were lapping water from the pool. One wolf, long and lean and gray, advanced cautiously, in a friendly manner, and Buck recognized the wild brother with whom he had run for a night and a day. He was whining softly, and, as Buck whined, they touched noses.

2170   Then an old wolf, gaunt and battle-scarred, came forward. Buck writhed his lips into the preliminary of a snarl, but sniffed noses with him. Whereupon the old wolf sat down, pointed nose at the moon, and broke out the long wolf howl. The others sat down and howled. And now the call came to Buck in unmistakable accents. He, too, sat down and howled. This over, he came out of his angle and the pack crowded around him,

2175 sniffing in half-friendly, half-savage manner. The leaders lifted the yelp of the pack and sprang away into the woods. The wolves swung in behind, yelping in chorus. And Buck ran with them, side by side with the wild brother, yelping as he ran.

And here may well end the story of Buck. The years were not many when the Yeehats noted a change in the breed of timber wolves; for some were seen with splashes

2180 of brown on head and muzzle, and with a rift of white centring down the chest. But more remarkable than this, the Yeehats tell of a Ghost Dog that runs at the head of the pack. They are afraid of this Ghost Dog, for it has cunning greater than they, stealing from their camps in fierce winters, robbing their traps, slaying their dogs, and defying their bravest hunters.

2185 Nay, the tale grows worse. Hunters there are who fail to return to the camp, and hunters there have been whom their tribesmen found with throats slashed cruelly open and with wolf prints about them in the snow greater than the prints of any wolf. Each fall, when the Yeehats follow the movement of the moose, there is a certain valley which they never enter. And women there are who become sad when the word goes over the

2190 fire of how the Evil Spirit came to select that valley for an abiding-place.

In the summers there is one visitor, however, to that valley, of which the Yeehats do not know. It is a great, gloriously coated wolf, like, and yet unlike, all other wolves. He crosses alone from the smiling timber land and comes down into an open space among the trees. Here a yellow stream flows from rotted moose-hide sacks and sinks

2195 into the ground, with long grasses growing through it and vegetable mould overrunning it and hiding its yellow from the sun; and here he muses for a time, howling once, long and mournfully, ere he departs.

But he is not always alone. When the long winter nights come on and the wolves follow their meat into the lower valleys, he may be seen running at the head of the pack

2200 through the pale moonlight or glimmering borealis, leaping gigantic above his fellows, his great throat a-bellow as he sings a song of the younger world, which is the song of the pack.

FINIS

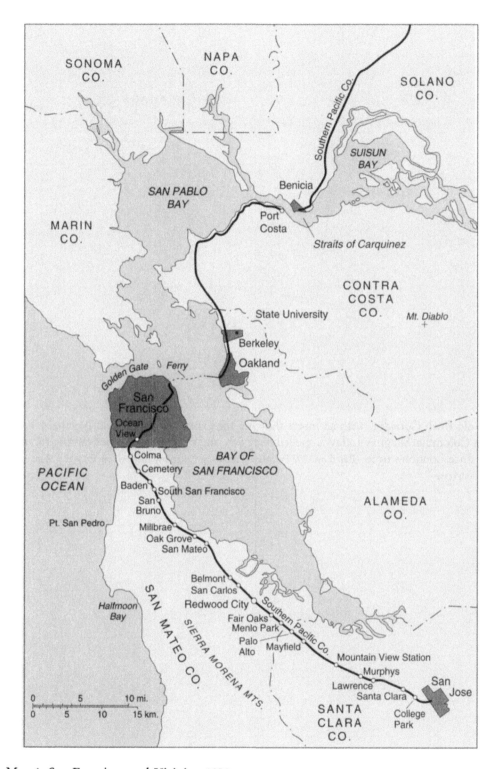

Map 1. San Francisco and Vicinity, 1898. (From *Rand McNally & Company's Indexed Atlas of the World,* © 1898 by Rand McNally, R.L. 95-S-250, 357)

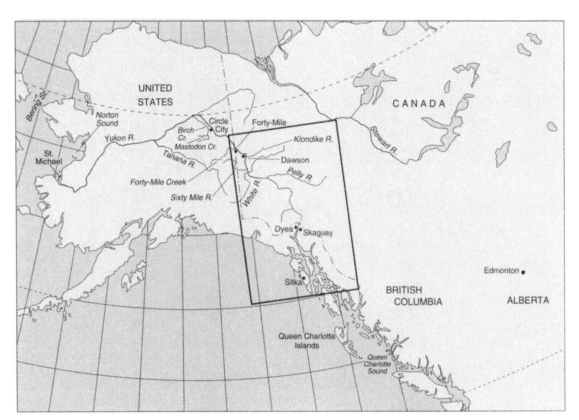

Map 2. The Gold Rush Corridor, with an insert showing the Canadian Yukon and Northern Territory of British Columbia. Skaguay today is spelled Skagway, and other place-names on maps 2 and 3 have changed since London's time. (Based on 1897 Province Publishing Company map, Geography and Maps Division, Library of Congress)

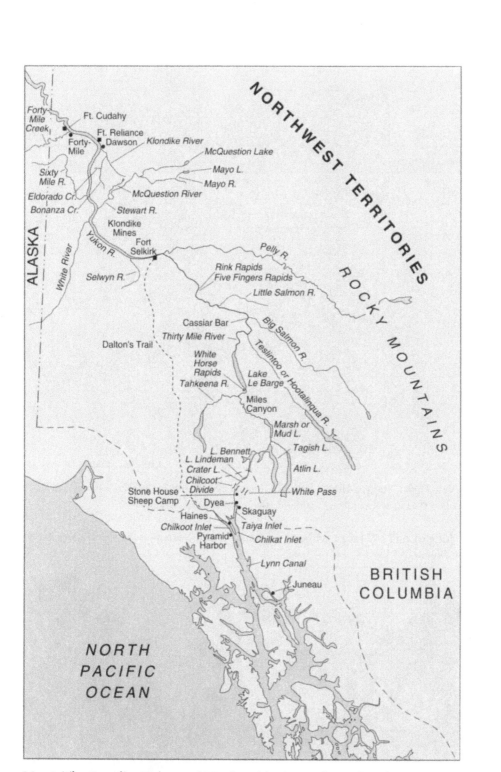

Map 3. The Canadian Yukon and Northern Territory of British Columbia, as described in Jack London's *The Call of the Wild*. London's Lake Le Barge is today Lake Laberge; McQuestion Lake and River are today spelled McQuesten. (Based on 1897 Province Publishing Company map, Geography and Maps Division, Library of Congress)

Fig. 1. New Park ("Judge Miller's Place"). (Reproduced from the *San Jose Daily Mercury*, 15 May 1892, courtesy of the California State Library, California Section, Sacramento, California)

Fig. 2. Judge Bond's ("Judge Miller's") House. (Photo courtesy of the Huntington Library, San Marino, California)

Fig. 3. On the left are Marshall and Louis Bond with their dog Jack ("Buck"). (Photo courtesy of the Huntington Library, San Marino, California)

Fig. 4. Healy & Wilson's Store, Dyea, Alaska (circa 1897). (Photo courtesy of the Yukon Archives/Vogee Collection, no. 103)

Fig. 5. Dog Team and Sled with Gee-Pole. (Photo courtesy of the Special Collections Division, University of Washington Libraries, neg. no.: Goetzman 3013)

Fig. 6. Chilkoot and Petterson Passes. (Photo courtesy of the Special Collections Division, University of Washington Libraries, neg. no.: Hegg 101)

Fig. 7. "Over the Bench Ice of Thirty Mile River." (Photo courtesy of the Everett D. Graff Collection, Newberry Library; reproduced in Palmer, *In the Klondike*, facing p. 26)

Fig. 8. Dawson City, Yukon (circa 1898). (Photo courtesy of the Special Collections Division, University of Washington Libraries, neg. no.: Hegg 742)

Fig. 9. "Gold Miners at Work." Miners had to burn their way down through the permafrost to bedrock, where the gold, if there was any, would be found. A fire roars in one shaft while the miners clear the other. (Charles Bramble, *Klondike: A Manual for Goldseekers* [New York: R. F. Fenno, 1897], facing 208; courtesy of the Edward E. Ayer Collection, Newberry Library)

Fig. 10. A Poling Boat. (Photo courtesy of the Charles Bunnell Collection, Charles E. Bunnell Album 1, no. 58-1026-166 9N, Archives, Alaska and Polar Regions Department, University of Alaska Fairbanks)

Fig. 11. "Looking Down the Canyon, Fortymile River." (Photo courtesy of the Edward E. Ayer Collection, Newberry Library; reproduced in Sola, *Klondyke: Truth and Facts*, facing 2)

Notes

1. "INTO THE PRIMITIVE"

Epigraph: "Old longings nomadic leap"
This is the first quatrain of "Atavism," an eight-stanza poem by John Myers O'Hara (1874–1944) published in the *Bookman* literary magazine in November 1902, only a month before London began writing *The Call of the Wild*. London and O'Hara, who did not know each other prior to 1903, eventually became correspondents and friends.

Line 1: Buck
London acknowledged in a letter to Klondike acquaintance Marshall Bond that he had based Buck on Bond's dog Jack, an animal that had much impressed London in the North. The dog was a mixed-breed—a St. Bernard and some kind of collie or shepherd. London said he selected the name Buck because it was "stronger" than Bright, another name he had considered (see fig. 3).

Lines 1–3: "trouble was brewing . . . from Puget Sound to San Diego"
Puget Sound is in on the northern Washington coast; San Diego is in southern California. Because of the huge demand for sled dogs in the Yukon, dogs were being stolen all along the West Coast.

Line 5: "booming the find"
Railway and shipping companies were heavily advertising the discovery of gold in the Klondike, encouraging people to join the adventure.

Line 8: "the . . . Santa Clara Valley"
Just south of San Francisco the enormous Santa Clara Valley extends 1,250 square miles, larger than Rhode Island. In London's day publicists for the valley claimed it had some of the richest ranch and orchard land in the world.

Lines 8–36: "Judge Miller's place"
London based his judge on Judge Hiram Gilbert Bond (1838–1906), whose sons, Louis and Marshall, had met London in the Klondike in 1897. For a time Judge Bond owned New Park, a large ranch in Santa Clara. Illustrations of the property from the era leave little doubt that London, who had been a guest of the Bonds in mid-October 1901, based "Judge Miller's place" on the Bond ranch. (See figures 1 and 2.) Today what remains of the ranch is a Carmelite monastery.

Line 16: "artesian well"
Artesian wells, which were common in the Santa Clara Valley, permit access to underground water that is overlaid by rock. Boring through the rock allows the pressure of the stream to force the water to rise through a pipe to the surface.

Line 30: "Mollie and Alice, the Judge's daughters"
Judge Bond's daughters-in-law were named Amy and Mary (also called "Mollie").

Lines 39–40: "Shep . . . a Scotch shepherd dog"
Shep was the name of one of Jack London's own boyhood dogs. "Scotch shepherd dog" is not the name of any breed recognized by the American Kennel Club. London probably meant some kind of collie.

Line 48: "Klondike"
The word "Klondike" probably derives from an American Indian word (*thron-diuck*) whose pronunciation was so difficult for speakers of English that the easier "Klondike" was soon substituted. The Indian word, which means "hammer-water," refers to the sounds made by American Indians as they set up their salmon nets.

Lines 51–52: "Chinese lottery"
Popular in the San Francisco Bay area, the lottery required players to guess which Chinese characters would be drawn each night from a group of eighty. For one dollar players could purchase ten characters. Five correct guesses earned $2; all ten, $3,000. Jack London's mother was a frequent but unlucky player.

Lines 55–56: "the Judge was at a meeting of the Raisin Growers' Association, and the boys were busy organizing an athletic club"
The principal fruit crop in the Santa Clara Valley was prunes, not raisins.

Judge Bond was founder and president of the California Cured Fruit Association. On the night that London visited the Bonds (15 October 1901), Judge Bond was in fact addressing a group of fruit growers. And Louis Bond, who was president of the newly formed Garden City Athletic Club in San Jose (his father also was a member), was attending to club business.

Line 59: "flag station known as College Park"
At a flag station trains do not stop unless signalled. College Park was the 432-acre tract of land between San Jose and Santa Clara where the University of the Pacific first opened its doors. For more than a century there has been a train depot near College Park. In London's day it was owned by the Southern Pacific and was only blocks away from the home of two of his friends, Ted and Mabel Applegarth. Today it is a stop on the Caltrain line. The depot is about three miles from the old Judge Bond ranch and about fifty miles from San Francisco—two hours by train in 1897.

Line 94: "'sou'"
A French coin of small value.

Line 96: "'squarehead'"
A derogatory term for Scandinavians, who were believed to be "thick-headed" and gullible.

Line 100: "'pull your freight'"
A railway expression meaning "to depart."

Line 121: "ferry steamer"
Buck spent the night in San Francisco before his passage across the Bay on one of the great steam-powered ferryboats that operated before the bridges were built. The trip cost passengers ten cents and took about twenty minutes.

Line 122: "a great railway depot"
This was the "Oakland Mole," a pier erected on a rock-fill out into the Bay. It featured a huge Victorian-style train shed that housed fourteen tracks.

Line 123: "for two days and nights this express car was dragged along"
In 1897 a rail journey from Oakland to Seattle took almost exactly two days and two nights.

Line 141: "they bundled him off the train at Seattle"
During the Klondike Gold Rush, Seattle became one of the principal points of departure for the gold seekers. In the city there were at least four large dog-training schools of the sort that the man in the red sweater operates.

Line 182: "'cayuses'"
A word for a horse (or wild horse) that originated among the Cayuse Indians of Oregon and Washington.

Line 188: "'ruction'"
A slang term for a disturbance or loud quarrel, probably from *insurrection.*

Line 190: "'all 'll go well and the goose hang high'"
This expression—which means "things will be all right"—was perhaps originally "the goose honks high" because migrating geese supposedly fly higher in good weather. Another possibility is that the expression derives from a southern game in which contestants on horseback attempt to grasp a well-greased goose hanging from the limb of a tree.

Line 217: "'Sacredam'"
"Sacredam" is Perrault's French-English equivalent of "holy damn" or "goddamn." London tried to persuade his editors to permit even more mild profanity in the text, but they were reluctant, fearing that such language would weaken sales to young people and to libraries.

Line 219: "'three hundred, and a present at that'"
The price of sled dogs soared during the Rush so that three hundred dollars was not an excessive amount for a fine dog.

Lines 223–24: "Canadian Government . . . despatches"
Worried about the tens of thousands of people rushing into the Yukon, the Canadian government hired men like Perrault and François to carry urgent messages to and from authorities in the Yukon interior.

Line 230: "the Narwhal"
No vessel named *Narwhal* participated in the Gold Rush. Perhaps London was thinking of the steam whaler by that name whose home port was San Francisco. Later that ship was sold to Warner Brothers and used as the *Pequod* in the 1926 film version of *Moby-Dick* called *The Sea Beast.* One of London's personal photograph albums contains a cutout of a newspaper article about and drawing of this *Narwhal.*

Line 233: "half-breed"
A derogatory term for a person of mixed parentage, usually American Indian and Caucasian.

Line 238: "the 'tween-decks"
Any space between the decks of a ship.

Line 239: "a big, snow-white fellow from Spitzbergen"
Spitzbergen is a group of islands in the Arctic Ocean, north of Norway. Travellers to the area in the nineteenth century commented on the white dogs common on the islands.

Line 240: "a Geological Survey into the Barrens"
The Barrens (or Barren Grounds or Barren Lands or Great Barrens) is a desolate region of tundra

west of Hudson Bay. The Geological Survey of Canada sponsored two highly publicized expeditions into the region in 1894 and 1895.

Lines 251–52: "Queen Charlotte Sound"
Much of the journey by sea from Seattle to Alaska—the "Inside Passage"—is sheltered by islands, permitting ships to avoid contact with the mighty northern Pacific. However, at Queen Charlotte Sound, on the coast of British Columbia, ships do encounter the open ocean. The passage can be very rough. The sound was named for the wife of England's King George III, who had sponsored the exploration of the area.

Line 255: "day and night the ship throbbed to the tireless pulse of the propeller"
The voyage from Seattle to Juneau, Alaska, took from four to seven days.

Line 265: "it was his first snow"
Snow fell only twice in the Santa Clara Valley between 1876 and 1896.

II. "THE LAW OF CLUB AND FANG"

Line 266: "the Dyea beach"
Dyea (pronounced "die-EE") was originally a Chilkat-Tlingit Indian fishing village about 100 miles north of Juneau, Alaska. The name means "carrying place," which is appropriate since Dyea sat at the foot of the Chilkoot Pass. During the Gold Rush, Dyea was a bustling beach town with a population around 10,000, but when the railroad decided to establish its terminus at nearby Skagway, Dyea quickly died, and today it is once again wilderness.

Line 276: "the log store"
This is probably Healy & Wilson's, a trading post that was the only permanent structure in Dyea in the years before the Rush (see fig. 4).

Line 299–300: "an arrangement of straps and buckles. . . . a harness"
The dog-sled harnesses used during the Rush consisted of a collar with lines (or "traces") running along the side connecting the dogs to one another and to the sled.

Line 301: "a sled"
Constructed of ash and pine, the Yukon sleds were seven feet long, sixteen inches wide, about six inches high, and weighed (unloaded) about eighty pounds. The ash runners were covered with two inches of iron.

Line 305: "whip"
Mushers customarily used thirty-foot-long whips of plaited seal hide.

Line 306: "wheeler"
The wheeler (or wheel dog) is the dog closest to the sled. The term was originally used with horses, the wheel horse being the animal closest to the wheels of a wagon.

Line 309: "traces"
Traces (or reins) were fashioned from various materials—cloth, leather, caribou intestine, moose or seal hide.

Line 317: "Joe"
When *The Call of the Wild* was first published in the *Saturday Evening Post*, this name was spelled "Jo."

Line 332: "Sol-leks, which means the Angry One"
In Chinook Jargon, the trade language employed by the American Indians in the North, *sol-leks* does indeed mean "angry" or "angry one."

Line 388: "Dyea Cañon"
The trail from Dyea over the Coast Mountains follows the Taiya River as it tumbles down to the ocean. The Dyea (or Taiya) Canyon is about eight miles from the coast and remains a spectacular natural obstacle for hikers.

Line 398: "single file"
A tandem arrangement of dogs was preferred by mushers throughout the Rush (see fig. 5). Coastal Eskimos, however, employed a fan-shaped arrangement of their animals.

Lines 412–14: "up the Cañon, through Sheep Camp, past the Scales . . . and over the great Chilcoot Divide"
About five miles beyond the Dyea Canyon is Sheep Camp, a spot that some believe derived its name from use at one time as headquarters for hunters of mountain sheep. Three miles beyond Sheep Camp is a gravel ledge, known as the Scales, where packers would weigh their supplies before their final assault on the summit. The Chilcoot Pass—named for the American Indians who discovered and controlled it—is about 3,500 feet above sea level. Photographs of miners scaling the Chilcoot in endless lines are among the most familiar images of the Gold Rush era (see fig. 6).

Lines 416–18: "the huge camp at the head of Lake Bennett, where thousands of gold-seekers were building boats against the break-up of the ice in the spring"
Located about sixteen miles beyond the Chilcoot summit, Lake Bennett (named for James Gordon Bennett, publisher of the *New York Herald*) is twenty-six miles long and is among the lakes that form the source of the Yukon River. Called Kusooa ("narrow lake") by the American Indians, Bennett was the place where the gold seekers built boats to carry them and their supplies the remaining 530 miles down the Yukon River to Dawson City and the goldfields.

Lines 421–23: "That day they made forty miles, the trail being packed; but . . . for many days to follow, they broke their own trail . . . and made poorer time. . . . Perrault travelled ahead of the team, packing the snow with webbed shoes"

Forty miles per day is well within the normal rate of dogsleds on a packed trail. François and Perrault are here employing the common method of travel by dog team: One person runs ahead, packing down the trail with snowshoes, while the partner steers the sled.

Line 424: "guiding the sled at the gee-pole"

Extending from the front of the sled on the right (or gee) side was the gee pole, a device used for steering and control. It was about six feet long, three inches thick, and reached to the musher's shoulder (see fig. 5).

Lines 431–32: "the pound and a half of sun-dried salmon, which was his ration"

For generations the American Indians fed themselves and their dogs the dried flesh of the Chinook salmon that swam up the Yukon River each year to spawn. The fish can grow to nearly five feet in length and weigh as much as 125 pounds.

Lines 441 and 444: Pike and Dub

These are two of the more aptly named dogs on the team. A *piker* is one who shirks responsibilities, and *dub* was slang for someone who does things awkwardly or stupidly.

Lines 471–74: "He learned to bite the ice out with his teeth when it collected between his toes; and when he was thirsty and there was a thick scum of ice over the water hole, he would break it by rearing and striking it with stiff fore legs. His most conspicuous trait was an ability to scent the wind and forecast it a night in advance."

All of these activities—except for the ice-breaking—were also recorded by other Northland writers.

III. "THE DOMINANT PRIMORDIAL BEAST"

Line 505: "Lake Le Barge"

This thirty-mile-long lake—immortalized by Robert Service in his poem "The Cremation of Sam McGee"—was named by explorer William H. Dall in 1870 for Michael Laberge, who had been involved in the 1865 attempt to string a telegraph line across Alaska and the Bering Strait. Laberge never saw the lake that bears his name. American Indians in the region called it Kluk-tas-si, a name that has never been satisfactorily translated.

Line 505: "a wind that cut like a white-hot knife"

Laberge is notorious for its fierce winds. On 30 September 1897, Jack London and his partners were forced to pull into a cove to avoid destruction by a gale on the lake.

Lines 506–7: "at their backs rose a perpendicular wall of rock"
In some places steep cliffs rise from the rocky shores of Lake Laberge.

Line 522: "'by Gar!'"
This is an Anglo-French corruption of "By God!"

Line 531: "some Indian village"
During the Rush there was a small encampment of impoverished Tagish Indians near Lake Laberge.

Lines 571–74: "The huskies had chewed through the sled lashings. . . . and even two feet of lash from the end of François's whip"
Huskies have a legendary capacity to eat anything "remotely eatable." Northland writers have recorded huskies ingesting pieces of harness, fur clothing, boots, straw, candles, soap, a whip, gloves, a hairbrush, and the plastic cages used to transport the animals.

Lines 578–79: "four hundred miles of trail still between him and Dawson"
The distance is approximately correct. Dawson City (named for George Mercer Dawson [1841– 1901], a Canadian geologist who was one of the most respected men in the North) is located at the confluence of the Yukon and Klondike Rivers. The town was staked out in August 1896 by Joe Ladue, who correctly anticipated the arrival of the Gold Rush stampede. Ladue erected a sawmill and made a fortune. At the height of the Rush, Dawson boasted a population of about thirty thousand and billed itself as "the Paris of the North." Today Dawson City's population has dwindled to about 700 (see fig. 8).

Lines 583–604: "The Thirty Mile River was wide open. . . . Six days of exhausting toil were required to cover those thirty terrible miles. . . . A dozen times, Perrault, nosing the way, broke through the ice bridges, being saved by the long pole he carried. . . . He skirted the frowning shores on rim ice. . . . Once the sled broke through. . . . there was no escape except up the cliff."
The Thirtymile River is actually a thirty-mile section of the Yukon River between Lake Laberge and the mouth of the Teslin (or Hootalinqua) River. Because the water is so rough, the section freezes more slowly than the more placid segments, forcing travellers by dog team to exercise extreme caution on its unpredictable surface. "Rim ice" is the ice closest to the shore (see fig. 7).

Line 610: "the Hootalinqua and good ice"
Hootalinqua (American Indian for "where the two big waters meet") is the older name for the river now known as the Teslin ("long, narrow water"). An even earlier American Indian name was Nas-A-Thane ("no salmon").

Lines 612–14: "thirty-five miles to the Big Salmon . . . thirty-five more to the Little Salmon . . . forty miles [more], which brought them well up toward the Five Fingers"
The mouth of the Big Salmon River is exactly thirty-five river miles from the mouth of the Hootalin-

qua; the mouth of the Little Salmon is exactly thirty-five farther; forty more miles would put the team only about twenty-four miles short of Five Finger Rapids. The names Big Salmon and Little Salmon are English translations of American Indian words that refer to the size of the fish in the waters.

Five Finger Rapids was the last spot of real danger on the float downriver to Dawson City. From overhead, large rocks in the river resemble the broken fingers of a huge hand.

Lines 620–23: "sacrificed the tops of his own moccasins to make four moccasins for Buck. . . . [who] lay on his back, his four feet waving appealingly in the air"
Northland travellers frequently wore high-top leather moccasins reaching to midcalf. Booties are common protective gear for sled dogs, whose feet can be shredded by rough, icy trails.

Lines 626–34: "at the Pelly one morning . . . Dolly . . . went suddenly mad. . . . [Buck] plunged through the wooded breast of the island, . . . crossed a back channel filled with rough ice to another island, gained a third island."
Named for Sir John Henry Pelly, British governor of the Hudson's Bay Company, the Pelly River enters the Yukon River at a spot where there are indeed many islands.

Line 644: "teams"
The *Saturday Evening Post* edition of the novel has "team" here, which is the correct word. "Teams" is a typographical error.

Line 672–73: "Pike, the malingerer, did not appear. He was securely hidden in his nest under a foot of snow."
Other Northland writers confirm that some dilatory dogs will hide at harness-up time.

Lines 699–700: "in the night their jingling bells still went by"
As early as the eighteenth century, Hudson's Bay Company voyageurs attached belled harnesses to their teams, believing the bells kept their dogs in good spirits.

Line 705: "the aurora borealis flaming coldly overhead"
The skies over Dawson City provided many spectacular displays of the Northern Lights for the gold seekers.

Lines 716–17: "they dropped down the steep bank by the Barracks to the Yukon Trail, and pulled for Dyea and Salt Water"
The Barracks were the headquarters of the North-west Mounted Police situated on the steep bank of the Yukon River at Dawson. (*Yukon* is an American Indian word meaning "the greatest" or "great river.")

The frozen surface of the Yukon River was the Yukon Trail—two thousand miles or so of sled trail. Upriver from Dawson, the trail led to Dyea or Skagway and the ocean ("Salt Water"). London has made a minor error here: They are headed for Skagway, not Dyea.

Lines 722–23: "the police had arranged in two or three places deposits of grub for dog and man"
Throughout the Rush, the North-west Mounted Police worked to establish way stations along the Yukon Trail; eventually, relief stops were available at thirty-mile intervals.

Line 724: "they made Sixty Mile, which is a fifty-mile run"
The Sixtymile River earned its name because of its distance from Fort Reliance, a trading post established in 1874. The mouth of the Sixtymile is about forty-seven miles from Dawson City.

Line 748: "at the mouth of the Tahkeena"
Takhini is a Tagish Indian word for "mosquito river," an extremely appropriate name to judge from numerous published accounts of travellers.

However, London has made an error here: The team could not be at the mouth of the Takhini. In subsequent pages he mentions that the team is at Rink Rapids, a spot about 220 miles upriver from the Takhini, farther back on the Yukon Trail.

Lines 748–49: "a snowshoe rabbit"
The snowshoe hare (*Lepus americanus*) was named because of its large hind feet, which can measure nearly six inches long, and its widely spread toes. The hares are dark brown in summer, but don a protective white coat in winter.

Lines 749–51: "A hundred yards away was a camp of the Northwest Police, with fifty dogs, huskies all, who joined the chase."
There was not a North-west Mounted Police post near the mouth of the Takhini at this time.

IV. "WHO HAS WON TO MASTERSHIP"

Line 854: "'Chook!'"
This is a Tlingit word meaning "go away" or "quick."

Line 910: "Rink Rapids"
Frederick Schwatka, who named many of the places in the Upper Yukon during his expedition in 1883, named the entire series of rapids near and including the Five Finger Rapids for Dr. Henry Rink, an authority on Greenland. However, travellers soon used the name "Rink" only for the somewhat tamer rapids about six miles downstream from Five Finger.

Line 911: "two native huskies, Teek and Koona"
Teek is a Tlingit word meaning "ice"; *Koona* is Cree for "snow."

Lines 917–18: "the temperature dropped to fifty below zero"
Such frigid temperatures are not uncommon in the bitter Yukon winters.

Lines 920–21: "they covered in one day going out what had taken them ten days coming in"
In lines 584–85 London tells us this portion of the trail took six days, not ten.

Lines 921–22: "In one run they made a sixty-mile dash from the foot of Lake Le Barge to the White Horse Rapids."
Approximately sixty miles below Lower Laberge, the Whitehorse Rapids were the bane of river travellers in the early days of the Rush. Named because the whitecaps resembled the flying manes of horses, the rapids no longer exist because a nearby dam has covered them with the waters of Lake Schwatka.

Line 923: "Marsh, Tagish, and Bennett (seventy miles of lakes)"
Depending on the route François and Perrault took across these lakes, the distance was approximately seventy miles from Marsh Lake to the settlement at Bennett.

Schwatka named Marsh Lake (called Mud Lake by many of the miners) for Professor Othniel Charles Marsh of Yale University; Tagish ("place where the geese sit down") was named by and for the American Indians in the region.

Line 925: "White Pass"
Named by Dominion land surveyor William Ogilvie for Sir Thomas White, Canadian minister of the interior, the pass was surveyed in 1887 by William "Billie" Moore, who first crossed it on 6 June 1887 with his Tagish companion, Skookum Jim Mason.

Line 926: "Skaguay"
Only a few miles south along the Alaska coast from Dyea, Skagway was for a year or so in stiff competition with its neighbor for Gold Rush business. Most historians of the region agree that the name came from a Tlingit word, *skagua* or *skagus,* meaning "home of the north wind"; some argue for another Tlingit word, *sch-kawai* ("end of the salt water").

In the early days of the Rush, the name of the town was spelled as London spells it—ending in *uay;* however, the name is now officially Skagway—with a *w.*

Line 927: "It was a record run. Each day for fourteen days they had averaged forty miles."
François and Perrault's fourteen-day trip was well within the range of a record run for the winter.

Line 928: "threw chests"
After their record run François and Perrault, chests puffed out with pride, swagger up and down the streets of Skagway.

Lines 930–32: "Then three or four western bad men aspired to clean out the town, were riddled like pepper-boxes for their pains, and public interest turned to other idols."

It is unknown if London is referring to any specific shoot-out, but throughout the Rush, Skagway was a wild, lawless town. Virtually every visitor to the town in the early days commented on its riotous, dangerous character. Because Skagway was on American soil, the North-west Mounted Police had no jurisdiction, and the U.S. authorities were ineffectual.

A pepper box is a small box with holes in the top for sprinkling pepper.

Line 946: "pitched the flies"

A "fly" is a primitive shelter—a variety of tent. In his story "Where the Trail Forks," London describes it as "a sheet of canvas stretched between two trees and angling at forty-five degrees. This caught the radiating heat from the fire and flung it down upon the skin."

Lines 964–89: Buck's vision in the fire

London was fascinated by "ancestral memories." *Before Adam,* his 1907 novel of prehistoric life, employs a similar device: An unnamed narrator, while studying evolution, realizes the dreams he has been having are actually memories of an ancient ancestor named Big-Tooth.

Line 1015: Cassiar Bar

Cassiar is a corruption of the native word *kaska,* which was the name given to some American Indians living in northern British Columbia and also their word for "creek." Cassiar Bar is a large sandbar in the Yukon River, about eight miles upstream from the mouth of the Big Salmon River. In 1886 four prospectors made a small gold strike on the bar, and for a while it featured a sizeable settlement. But larger strikes elsewhere, especially on the Klondike, soon made Cassiar little more than a landmark.

Jack London became intimately familiar with Cassiar Bar on 3 October 1897 when his boat ran aground on it.

Dave's struggle had been impressive: Cassiar Bar is about 340 miles from Dawson City.

V. "THE TOIL OF TRACE AND TRAIL"

Line 1063: "the Salt Water Mail"

Mail back and forth from Dawson City to the ocean-going ships at Dyea and Skagway ("Salt Water") was irregular, but the North-west Mounted Police, who carried the mail, attempted to keep a twice-monthly schedule.

Line 1090: "Hudson Bay dogs"

London is referring to the variety of husky found in the vicinity of Hudson Bay.

Lines 1098–99: "a big Colt's revolver and a hunting-knife"
Business was booming throughout the Rush for manufacturers of firearms and other weapons. London is referring to a revolver made by Colt's Patent Fire Arms Manufacturing Company (now simply "Colt's Manufacturing") of Hartford, Connecticut. The company advertised heavily in West Coast magazines during the Rush.

Line 1153: "'Rest be blanked,' said Hal"
"Blanked," a euphemism for "damned," derives from the publishing practice of substituting blank spaces for proscribed words.

Line 1183–84: "chief thoroughfare"
The main street of Skagway was—and is—Broadway, named because it was eighty feet wide, twenty feet wider than the other streets in town.

Line 1189: "the Long Trail"
London is referring to the 600-mile trail between Dawson City and Skagway or Dyea.

Line 1192: "'Good Lord, do you think you're travelling on a Pullman?'"
The Pullman Palace Car Company, founded by George Pullman (1831–97), was for many years the principal manufacturer of luxury railroad cars in the world.

Line 1222: "Q.E.D."
This abbreviation for the Latin phrase *quod erat demonstrandum* ("which was to be demonstrated") is traditionally placed at the end of mathematical proofs.

Lines 1309–10: "a toothless old squaw"
Canada's Department of Indian Affairs reported that there were at this time (spring 1898) about 200 Canadian Natives in the vicinity of Five Finger Rapids.

Although *squaw* is the English spelling of the Narragansett Indian word for "woman," the word now has derogatory, racist connotations.

Lines 1312–13: "this hide . . . stripped from the starved horses of the cattlemen six months back"
London is alluding to an actual event—the slaughter of more than two thousand cattle and horses that had been driven over the Dalton Trail, which began at Pyramid Harbor, Alaska, and ended at the mouth of the Pelly River (see map 2). Although the Dalton Trail had sufficient grass in the summer to feed the horses of the cattlemen, the Yukon interior did not, and so the cattlemen slaughtered their horses at the Pelly site. Today Yukon River maps identify a spot near the mouth of the Pelly as Slaughterhouse Slough.

Lines 1359–60: "The Yukon was straining to break loose the ice that bound it down."
In 1898—the year that Hal, Charles, and Mercedes were on the river trail—the ice broke at Dawson City on 8 May.

Line 1366: "John Thornton"
When Jack London left the Klondike in the spring of 1898, he floated down the Yukon River to the Bering Sea with two other men, one of whom was John Thorson. It is likely that London is here honoring his old Yukon companion.

Line 1367: "White River"
Spilling from the west into the Yukon River some eighty miles upriver from Dawson City, the White River was named for its color by Robert Campbell of the Hudson's Bay Company in 1851. American Indian names were Sand River or Copper River. The White, loaded with glacial silt and volcanic ash, is indeed milky in color. Because of the sediment the Yukon River waters are no longer potable between the White River and the ocean—over 1,400 miles.

Line 1376: "rotten ice"
Also called "rotting ice," this is ice that is beginning to soften and break up.

VI. "FOR THE LOVE OF A MAN"

Line 1441: "John Thornton froze his feet"
Frozen feet were a common and deadly occurrence during the Rush. Travellers who broke through rotten ice had to scramble to build a fire to save their feet—and their lives—in the bitter subarctic cold.

Lines 1442–43: "to get out a raft of saw-logs for Dawson"
The demand for lumber and firewood was so high in Dawson City that many, having failed at mining or other enterprises, went up the creeks and streams draining into the Yukon, felled trees, formed huge rafts, and floated them down to Dawson to sell to the sawmills. Jack London himself did this in the spring of 1898, earning money to purchase medicine for his scurvy and supplies for the journey home.

Line 1450: "Skeet and Nig"
Skeet was the name of a little terrier owned by the wife of one of London's best friends, poet George Sterling. Nig was a huge black dog owned by one of London's Yukon companions, Louis Savard.

It is possible that Savard, a French-Canadian, had named his big, lumbering dog Nigaud (French for "fool" or "simpleton"). A less sympathetic explanation is that the name is racist.

Lines 1549–50: "ere they swung the raft into the big eddy by the saw-mill at Dawson"
There is a well-known eddy (abrupt change in the current) near the spot where Joe Ladue erected his sawmill at Dawson City.

Lines 1555–56: "the head-waters of the Tanana"
Tanana (pronounced "TAN-uh-naw") is an American Indian word meaning "river trail." Thornton and his partners are heading into territory that many publications had suggested might be rich in gold deposits.

Line 1569: "Circle City"
Circle City, Alaska, was so named because it supposedly was located on the Arctic Circle, which in fact lies about fifty miles farther north. The comparatively modest strikes on nearby Birch Creek and its tributaries—$150,000 between 1892 and 1895—brought more people to Circle, and eventually it grew into a community more deserving of the name "city": By 1896 its population was 1,200. The Klondike strikes—some 300 miles upriver—ended Circle's brief period of prosperity, and by 1990 the U.S. Census recorded only 73 persons living in Circle—no longer City—Alaska.

Line 1570: "'Black' Burton"
The Klondike Gold Rush may have produced as many nicknames as nuggets. Swiftwater Bill, Salt-water Jack, Big Dick, Squaw-tamer, Jimmy the Pirate, Big Aleck, Jimmy the Tough, Pete the Pig, Buckskin Miller, Old Maiden, Shoemaker Brown, Mollie Fewclothes, Ethel the Moose, and the Evaporated Kid are among the more colorful.

The nickname "Black" generally indicated race, and it is possible that London based this character upon "Black" Bill, an actual African American bartender in Circle.

Line 1571: "tenderfoot"
London's use of this word—meaning "newcomer"—is surprising here, for throughout his Northland writing he prefers the Chinook Jargon synonym, *cheechako,* which was—and is—in general use in the region.

Line 1581: "a surgeon checked the bleeding"
It is unlikely that a surgeon would have been in Circle at this time in its history. As London himself had observed in his notes in late spring 1898, Circle was virtually abandoned. It is possible that the surgeon was not a licensed professional but someone skilled in the frontier arts of patching and stitching.

Line 1583: "A 'miners' meeting'"
In remote Alaska mining camps, and even in sizable settlements like Circle City, there was no law beyond that established and enforced by the residents themselves. When someone violated the codes of

decency or fairness—or when there was a dispute of some sort—the miners assembled to resolve the issue and to impose penalties ranging from banishment to whipping or hanging.

Line 1585: Alaska
Although the namers thought Alaska meant "great land," it comes from another Aleut word, *alaxsxaq*, which means "where the sea breaks its back."

Lines 1587–89: "the three partners were lining a long and narrow poling-boat down a bad stretch of rapids . . . snubbing with a thin Manila rope from tree to tree"
The long, narrow poling boats—up to thirty feet long—were popular on the Yukon waterways (see fig. 10). Travellers stood and propelled the boats with a long pole driven for leverage into the river bottom.

"Lining" and then "snubbing" a boat required a partner on shore to attach a rope—or line—to the boat, wrap it around a tree, and therewith control the vessel's progress in swift water.

Lines 1587–88: "a bad stretch of rapids on the Forty-Mile Creek"
Named for its distance from Fort Reliance, Fortymile River does have a set of bad rapids about eight miles upstream from where it flows into the Yukon River. Gold was first discovered on the Fortymile in September 1886, and for ten years there was an active mining community in the region. However, the discoveries on the Klondike—only about fifty miles away—dealt Fortymile a death blow.

Line 1650: "totem-pole"
The Tlingit Indians erected these family memorials at numerous locations along the coast of Alaska.

Line 1654: Eldorado Saloon
There was at the time of these events an Eldorado Saloon in Klondike City, just across the Klondike River from Dawson City. El Dorado was the legendary City of Gold sought by the Spaniards in the American Southwest (*dorado* means "golden" in Spanish). The name was given to a variety of landmarks throughout the Klondike. Eldorado Creek, for example, was the richest creek ever discovered on the planet.

Line 1659: "'Buck can start a thousand pounds.'"
Modern pulling records for a single dog are about two thousand pounds, and so Buck's feat is certainly plausible.

Line 1661: "a Bonanza King"
Bonanza comes from the Spanish word meaning "fair weather and calm sea" or "prosperity." The word gradually drifted into English and came to mean a rich deposit of ore, or great and sudden wealth or good fortune.

The use of *king* in this fashion was a Northland way to refer to someone who had struck it rich. Thus a "Bonanza King" had a rich claim on Bonanza Creek.

Lines 1665–66: "a sack of gold dust the size of a bologna sausage"
Because gold dust was the medium of exchange in Dawson City during the Rush, every place of business had a scale; every miner carried a "poke" (a sack of dust). London continued to carry his throughout his life.

The size and nature of the wager on Buck are not extraordinary. Many published memoirs of the Rush contain accounts of wild betting on events ranging from roulette to spitting accuracy.

Lines 1678–79: "Jim O'Brien, a Mastodon King"
Jim O'Brien had a rich claim on Mastodon Creek, part of the Birch Creek drainage system in the Circle City mining region. The Birch Creek strikes came in 1893, and Mastodon, named in 1894 by miners who had found fossil mastodon bones in it, was among the richest of the creeks in the region.

Lines 1719–20: "a king of the Skookum Benches"
On 22 March 1897, Joseph Goldsmith named two of Bonanza's tributaries "Little Skookum" and "Big Skookum." *Skookum* is Chinook Jargon for "good" or "strong" or "powerful." It is unclear, however, if Goldsmith named the creeks for Skookum Jim Mason, a Tagish Indian who participated in the original strike on Bonanza Creek, or merely intended the Chinook Jargon word to refer to the richness of the gold deposits.

A bench claim is on the side or top of a hill in an ancient, not a current, creek bed. A "king of the Skookum Benches" was a person who had a rich bench claim on the hill above Big or Little Skookum.

Lines 1740, 1744: "'Gee!'" "'Haw!'"
These commands for draft animals mean, respectively, "right" and "left."

VII. "THE SOUNDING OF THE CALL"

Line 1781–85: "a fabled lost mine . . . an ancient and ramshackle cabin"
Several "lost mines" in North America were called the "Lost Cabin"; none of them, however, were in Alaska or Canada.

Lines 1791–93: "They sledded seventy miles up the Yukon . . . the Stewart River . . . the Mayo . . . the McQuestion . . . until the Stewart itself became a streamlet, threading the upstanding peaks"
The mouth of the Stewart is almost exactly seventy miles upstream from Dawson City, where Buck has just won the bet. The "upstanding peaks" are the Mackenzie Mountains, named for Canada's second prime minister, Alexander Mackenzie (1822–92). They lie approximately two hundred miles east of Dawson. In 1851, Robert Campbell named the Stewart River for his Hudson's Bay Company colleague, Robert Green Stewart. The local American Indian name was Na-Chon-De—also the name of the people called Tutchone today. London knew this area well, for he had arrived there on

9 October 1897—barely beating freeze-up—and spent the winter on an island near the mouth of the Stewart.

The Mayo River was named by William Ogilvie for Kentuckian Alfred Mayo, an early Yukon explorer and trader who had once been a circus acrobat. The McQuesten River was named for LeRoy Napoleon "Jack" McQuesten (1836–1909), a partner of Mayo and Arthur Harper (another early Yukon explorer) and generally acknowledged as "the Father of the Yukon." The founder of trading posts and the grantor of credit—and the "King of Circle City"—McQuesten was one of the most beloved men in the North.

Line 1806: "burning holes through frozen muck and gravel and washing countless pans of dirt"
Throughout the Yukon, just below the surface, is permafrost—permanently frozen subsoil hard as concrete and yielding only grudgingly to a miner's pick and shovel. To determine if a claim had value, miners had to dig a shaft through the permafrost to bedrock—sometimes as much as one hundred feet down—where the gold, if there was any, would have settled. The miners, who built fires in their shafts to melt the permafrost, would not know their fortune until they had burned and dug to the bottom, a process that could take a month or longer (see fig. 9).

The pans used by the miners were twelve inches in diameter at the bottom and fifteen to sixteen inches across the top.

Lines 1808–9: "Summer arrived, and dogs and men packed on their backs"
It was common practice among the American Indians in the Northland to use their sled dogs as pack animals in the summer months; they could carry forty to sixty pounds.

Lines 1813–14: "the midnight sun"
In late June the sun is visible in arctic latitudes twenty-four hours a day.

Lines 1815–16: "in the shadows of glaciers picked strawberries and flowers as ripe and fair as any the Southland could boast"
This apparent anomaly of lush fruit and flowers growing in "the shadows of glaciers" is a well-documented Northland phenomenon. London, who left the Yukon in June 1898, had certainly seen the lushness of subarctic vegetation made possible by the long hours of sunshine and warm temperatures during Northland summers.

Lines 1826–28: "a long-barrelled flint-lock.... a Hudson Bay Company gun of the young days ... worth its height in beaver skins packed flat"
The Hudson's Bay Company (HBC), the oldest trading company in the world, received its charter from English King Charles II on 2 May 1670. In the eighteenth century the HBC began establishing trading posts in the interior of subarctic North America and enjoyed a virtual monopoly on trade with the American Indians for scores of years.

The trade items most desired by the American Indians were firearms—specifically, the flintlock muskets that London mentions. Quite an assortment of weapons was traded throughout the centuries, but they were easily identifiable as HBC guns because of the brass serpent trademark usually affixed to the stock of the rifles.

London's statement that a gun was worth "its height in beaver skins packed flat"—a common story in the Northland—is inaccurate: If the cost were based on a pile of pelts equal in height to the length of the gun, this would have resulted in a pile of about 300 pelts—far beyond the standard price of twelve pelts or so.

Line 1832: "placer"
A placer mine (pronounced "PLASS-ur") is a superficial gravel deposit—normally in the bed of a stream—containing particles of gold.

Line 1835: "the gold was sacked in moose-hide bags, fifty pounds to the bag"
Throughout the Rush, gold was $16 an ounce. At that rate each of the fifty-pound bags "piled like so much firewood outside" was worth $12,800. At today's rate of $400 an ounce, each sack would be worth about $320,000.

Line 1836: "the spruce-bough lodge"
Using branches of evergreens—both for temporary shelters and for bedding— was common in the Northland.

Line 1836: "like giants they toiled"
Although London no doubt meant to suggest here that Thornton and his partners worked extremely hard, there is another interpretation: In the late nineteenth century a "giant" was also a large pipe used to wash ore.

Line 1871: "niggerheads"
This offensive slang term for dark clumps of arctic vegetation was used in other Gold Rush publications.

Lines 2005–6: "the bull tossed his great palmated antlers, branching to fourteen points and embracing seven feet within the tips"
Contrary to London's depiction here, moose do not generally form herds in the fall of the year, nor do bulls have a "harem." However, the moose's antlers, which begin growing in April, would indeed have been at their full growth about this time—although the seven-foot antler span would be larger by three inches than the largest on record.

Line 2098: "The Yeehats"
There was no tribe of American Indians named Yeehat. London's decision to employ a fictitious tribe is consistent with Northland traditions, however, for it was common to hear tales of barbarous people living in remote and unexplored regions of the territory. At the time of the Rush there were tales

about fierce American Indians in the Mackenzie Mountains—the very region Thornton and his partners have entered. Although there were in fact very few violent encounters with American Indians during the Rush, newspapers warned the gold seekers about potential dangers.

Line 2120: "sluice boxes"
Designed to separate gold from gravel, each wooden sluice box was about twelve feet long, a foot wide, and eight to ten inches high. On the bottom were riffles (small strips of wood). Miners first shoveled gravel and dirt into the boxes, then poured on water, which washed away loose gravel and debris, leaving behind the heavier gold in the riffles.

Lines 2178–79: "the Yeehats noted a change in the breed of timber wolves"
Wolves and dogs can mate successfully, but in the hierarchy of a wolf pack only the "alpha," or highest-ranking, male breeds. Accordingly, the change noted by the Yeehats is further evidence of Buck's continuing dominance.

Bibliography

1. BY JACK LONDON

Burning Daylight. New York: Macmillan, 1910.

The Call of the Wild. New York: Macmillan, 1903.

"Chased by the Trail." *Youth's Companion,* 26 September 1907, 445–46.

Children of the Frost. New York: Macmillan, 1902.

The Complete Short Stories of Jack London. Edited by Earle Labor, Robert C. Leitz, III, and I. Milo Shepard. 3 vols. Stanford, Calif.: Stanford University Press, 1993.

A Daughter of the Snows. Philadelphia: J. B. Lippincott Co., 1902.

"The Economics of the Klondike." *Review of Reviews* 21 (January 1900): 70–74.

"The End of the Story." In *The Turtles of Tasman,* by Jack London, 221–65. New York: Macmillan, 1916.

The Faith of Men and Other Stories. New York: Macmillan, 1904.

"Finis." In *The Turtles of Tasman,* by Jack London, 184–220. New York: Macmillan, 1916.

"From Dawson to the Sea." *Buffalo Express,* 4 June 1899. In *Jack London's Tales of Adventure,* edited by Irving Shepard, 42–49. Garden City, N.Y.: Hanover House, 1956.

"The 'Fuzziness' of Hoockla-Heen." *Youth's Companion,* 3 July 1902, 333–34.

The God of His Fathers and Other Stories. New York: McClure, Phillips, 1901.

"The Gold Hunters of the North." *Atlantic* 92 (July 1903): 42–49. In *Revolution and Other Essays,* by Jack London. New York: Macmillan, 1910.

"Housekeeping in the Klondike." *Harper's Bazar,* 15 September 1900, 1227–32.

"Husky—the Wolf-Dog of the North." *Harper's Weekly,* 30 June 1900, 611.

"The King of Mazy May." *Youth's Companion,* 30 November 1899, 629–30.

The Letters of Jack London. Edited by Earle Labor, Robert C. Leitz, III, and I. Milo Shepard. 3 vols. Stanford: Stanford University Press, 1988.

"Like Argus of the Ancient Times." In *The Red One,* by Jack London, 89–141. New York: Macmillan, 1918.

Lost Face. New York: Macmillan, 1910.

Love of Life and Other Stories. New York: Macmillan, 1906.

"A Northland Miracle." *Youth's Companion,* 4 November 1926, 813–14. This story was written in 1900 but not published until the date cited.

"Pluck and Pertinacity." *Youth's Companion,* 4 January 1900, 2–3.

Scorn of Women. New York: Macmillan, 1906.

"The Shrinkage of the Planet." *Chautauquan* 31 (September 1900): 609–12. In *Revolution and Other Essays,* by Jack London, 141–57. New York: Macmillan, 1910.

Smoke Bellew. New York: Century, 1912.

The Son of the Wolf. Boston: Houghton Mifflin, 1900.

"Thanksgiving on Slav Creek." *Harper's Bazar,* 24 November 1900, 1879–84.

"Through the Rapids on the Way to the Klondike." *Home,* June 1899. In *Jack London's Tales of Adventure,* edited by Irving Shepard, 39–42. Garden City, N.Y.: Hanover House, 1956.

"Up the Slide." *Youth's Companion,* 25 October 1906, 545.

White Fang. New York: Macmillan, 1906.

2. ABOUT JACK LONDON AND HIS WRITING

Benoit, Raymond. "Jack London's *The Call of the Wild.*" *American Quarterly* 20 (summer 1968): 246–48.

Berton, Pierre. Introduction to *The Call of the Wild,* by Jack London. Los Angeles: Ward Ritchie, 1960.

"Best Work of Jack London." *San Francisco Chronicle,* 2 August 1903, 32.

Bond, Marshall, Jr. *Judge Miller of Jack London's "The Call of the Wild."* Santa Barbara, Calif.: privately printed, 1980.

"Books New and Old." *Atlantic Monthly,* November 1903, 693–98.

"'The Call of the Wild,' by Jack London." *Athenaeum* 3957 (29 August 1903): 279.

Dickey, James. Introduction to *"The Call of the Wild," "White Fang," and Other Stories,* by Jack London. Edited by Andrew Sinclair. New York: Penguin, 1981.

Doctorow, E. L. Introduction to *The Call of the Wild,* by Jack London. Edited by Donald Pizer. New York: Vintage Library of America, 1990.

Doubleday, J. Stewart. *"The Call of the Wild."* *Reader* 2 (September 1903): 408–9. In *"The Call of the Wild," by Jack London: A Casebook,* edited by Earl J. Wilcox, 150–51. Chicago: Nelson-Hall, 1980.

Fadiman, Clifton. Afterword to *The Call of the Wild*, by Jack London, 127–28. New York: Macmillan, 1963.

Flink, Andrew. "*Call of the Wild:* Jack London's Catharsis." *Jack London Newsletter* 11 (1978): 12–19.

——. "'Call of the Wild': Parental Metaphor." *Jack London Newsletter* 7 (May–August 1974): 58–61. In *"The Call of the Wild" by Jack London: A Casebook*, edited by Earl J. Wilcox, 229–33. Chicago: Nelson-Hall, 1980.

Frey, Charles. "Contradiction in *The Call of the Wild*." *Jack London Newsletter* 12 (1979): 35–37.

Fusco, Richard. "On Primitivism in *The Call of the Wild*." *American Literary Realism* 20 (Fall 1987): 76–80.

Geismar, Maxwell. Introduction to *Jack London: Short Stories*. New York: Hill & Wang, 1960.

——. "Jack London: The Short Cut." In *Rebels and Ancestors: The American Novel, 1890–1915*, 139–216. Boston: Houghton Mifflin, 1953.

Gurian, Jay. "The Romantic Necessity in Literary Naturalism: Jack London." *American Literature* 38 (March 1966): 112–14. In *"The Call of the Wild," by Jack London: A Casebook*, edited by Earl J. Wilcox, 174–77. Chicago: Nelson-Hall, 1980.

Hamilton, David Mike. *"The Tools of My Trade": Annotated Books in Jack London's Library*. Seattle: University of Washington Press, 1986.

Hedrick, Joan D. *"The Call of the Wild."* In *Solitary Comrade: Jack London and His Work*, by Joan D. Hedrick, 94–111. Chapel Hill: University of North Carolina Press, 1982.

Jensen, Emil. "Jack London at Stewart River, 13 November 1926." Typed manuscript in Huntington Library, San Marino, Calif.

Kingman, Russ. *Jack London: A Definitive Chronology*. Middletown, Calif.: David Rejl, 1992.

——. *A Pictorial Life of Jack London*. New York: Crown, 1979.

Koenig, Jacqueline. "Jack London's *The Call of the Wild*." *Jack London Newsletter* 9 (1976): 127–29.

Labor, Earle. Introduction to *Great Short Works of Jack London*. New York: Harper & Row, 1965, 1970.

——. *Jack London*. New York: Twayne, 1974.

——. "Jack London." In *The Concise Dictionary of American Literary Biography*, vol. 2, *Realism, Naturalism, and Local Color, 1865–1877*, 270–91. Detroit: Gale Research, 1988.

——. "Jack London's *Mondo Cane*: 'Bâtard,' *The Call of the Wild*, and *White Fang*." In *Critical Essays on Jack London*, edited by Jacqueline Tavernier-Courbin, 114–30. Boston: G. K. Hall, 1983. Also in *"The Call of the Wild" by Jack London: A Casebook*, edited by Earl J. Wilcox, 202–16. Chicago: Nelson-Hall, 1980. These are revisions of an article originally published in *Jack London Newsletter* 1 (September–December 1967): 2–13.

Labor, Earle, and Robert C. Leitz, III. Introduction to *"The Call of the Wild," "White Fang," and Other Stories*, by Jack London. New York: Oxford University Press, 1990.

Labor, Earle, and Jeanne Campbell Reesman. *Jack London*. Rev. ed. New York: Twayne, 1994.

Lampson, Robin. "Some Sources of Jack London's Titles." *Pacific Historian* 20 (spring 1976): 4–7.

London, Charmian Kittredge. *The Book of Jack London*. 2 vols. New York: Century, 1921.

London, Joan. *Jack London and His Daughters.* Berkeley, Calif.: Heydey, 1990.

———. *Jack London and His Times: An Unconventional Biography.* Garden City, N.Y.: Doubleday, 1939. Reprint, Seattle: University of Washington Press, 1968.

Lundquist, James. *Jack London: Adventures, Ideas, and Fiction.* New York: Ungar, 1987.

Lynn, Kenneth S. "Jack London: The Brain Merchant." In *The Dream of Success: A Study of the Modern American Imagination,* by Kenneth S. Lynn, 75–118. Boston: Little, Brown, 1955.

McClintock, James I. *White Logic: Jack London's Short Stories.* Grand Rapids, Mich.: Wolf House, 1975.

Mann, John S. "The Theme of the Double in *The Call of the Wild.*" *Markham Review* 8 (fall 1978): 1–5.

Martin, Stoddard. "The Novels of Jack London." *Jack London Newsletter* 14 (May–August 1981): 48–71.

Maurice, Arthur Bartlett. "Jack London, 'The Call of the Wild.'" *Bookman* 18 (October 1903): 159–60.

Mitchill, Theodore C. Introduction to *The Call of the Wild,* by Jack London. New York: Macmillan, 1928.

Mott, Frank Luther. Introduction to *The Call of the Wild,* by Jack London. New York: Macmillan, 1928.

"A 'Nature' Story—*The Call of the Wild,* by Jack London." *Literary World* 34 (September 1903): 229. In *"The Call of the Wild," by Jack London: A Casebook,* edited by Earl J. Wilcox, 149. Chicago: Nelson-Hall, 1980.

Noel, Joseph. *Footloose in Arcadia: A Personal Record of Jack London, George Sterling, Ambrose Bierce.* New York: Carrick & Evans, 1940.

North, Dick. *Jack London's Cabin.* Whitehorse, Yukon: Willow, 1986.

Noto, Sal. "Jack London and the College Park Station." *San Jose Historical Association News* (January 1987): 7.

O'Connor, Richard. *Jack London: A Biography.* Boston: Little, Brown, 1964.

Paulsen, Gary. Introduction to *The Call of the Wild,* by Jack London. New York: Macmillan, 1994.

Perry, John. *Jack London: An American Myth.* Chicago: Nelson-Hall, 1981.

Pizer, Donald. Notes to *The Call of the Wild,* by Jack London, 101–102. New York: Vintage Library of America, 1990.

Reed, A. Paul. "Running with the Pack: Jack London's *The Call of the Wild* and Jesse Stuart's *Mongrel Mettle.*" *Jack London Newsletter* 18 (September–December 1985): 96–98.

Rothberg, Abraham. Introduction to *"The Call of the Wild" and "White Fang,"* by Jack London. New York: Bantam, 1981.

Seeyle, John. Introduction to *"White Fang" and "The Call of the Wild,"* by Jack London. New York: Signet, 1991.

Sinclair, Andrew. *Jack: A Biography of Jack London.* New York: Harper & Row, 1977.

Spinner, Jonathan H. "A Syllabus for the 20th Century: Jack London's 'The Call of the Wild.'" *Jack London Newsletter* 7 (May–August 1974): 73–78. In *"The Call of the Wild," by Jack London: A Casebook,* edited by Earl J. Wilcox, 234–42. Chicago: Nelson-Hall, 1980.

Stasz, Clarice. *American Dreamers: Charmian and Jack London.* New York: St. Martin's, 1988.

Stillé, Kate B. "Review of *The Call of the Wild.*" *Book News Monthly* 22 (September 1903): 7–10. In *"The Call of the Wild," by Jack London: A Casebook,* edited by Earl J. Wilcox, 157–60. Chicago: Nelson-Hall, 1980.

Stone, Irving. *Sailor on Horseback: The Biography of Jack London.* Boston: Houghton Mifflin, 1938. Reprint, New York: Signet, 1969.

Swain, Dwight. Afterword to *The Call of the Wild,* by Jack London, 107–14. New York: Aerie, 1986.

Thompson, Fred. "Diary of Yukon Experiences with Jack London, Mr. Shepard, Merritt Sloper, Jim Goodman, July–October 1897." Typed manuscript, Huntington Library, San Marino, Calif.

Upton, Ann. "The Wolf in London's Mirror." *Jack London Newsletter* 6 (September–December 1973): 111–18. In *"The Call of the Wild," by Jack London: A Casebook,* edited by Earl J. Wilcox, 193–201. Chicago: Nelson-Hall, 1980.

Walcutt, Charles Child. *Jack London.* University of Minnesota Pamphlets on American Writers, no. 57. Minneapolis: University of Minnesota Press, 1966.

———. "Jack London." In *Seven Novels in the American Naturalist Tradition: An Introduction.* Edited by Charles Child Walcutt, 131–67. Minneapolis: University of Minnesota Press, 1974.

———. "Jack London: Blond Beasts and Supermen." In *American Literary Naturalism, A Divided Stream,* 87–113. Minneapolis: University of Minnesota Press, 1956.

Walker, Franklin. Foreword to *"The Call of the Wild" and Selected Stories,* by Jack London. New York: Signet, 1960.

———. *Jack London and the Klondike: The Genesis of an American Writer.* San Marino, Calif.: Huntington Library, 1966.

Watson, Charles N. *The Novels of Jack London: A Reappraisal.* Madison: University of Wisconsin Press, 1983.

Wilcox, Earl J. "Jack London's Naturalism: The Example of *The Call of the Wild.*" *Jack London Newsletter* 20 (December 1969): 91–101. In *"The Call of the Wild," by Jack London: A Casebook,* edited by Earl J. Wilcox, 178–92. Chicago: Nelson-Hall, 1980.

Williams, Tony. *Jack London: The Movies.* Los Angeles, Calif.: David Rejl, 1992.

3. THE NORTHLAND: ALASKA, THE YUKON, AND THE GOLD RUSH

Adney, Edwin Tappan. *The Klondike Stampede.* New York: Harper & Brothers, 1900.

Berton, Pierre. *Drifting Home.* New York: Alfred A. Knopf, 1974.

———. *Klondike: The Last Great Gold Rush, 1896–1899.* Rev. ed. Toronto: McClelland & Stewart Limited, 1985.

———. *The Klondike Quest.* Boston: Little, Brown, 1983.

A Boater's Guide to the Upper Yukon River. Rev. ed. Anchorage: Alaska Northwest Publishing Co., 1976.

Bond, Marshall. "Klondike Diary." Autograph manuscript, Western Americana Collection, Beinecke Rare Book and Manuscript Library, Yale University, New Haven, Conn.

Bond, Marshall, Jr. *Gold Hunter: The Adventures of Marshall Bond.* Albuquerque: University of New Mexico Press, 1969.

Bruce, Miner Wait. *Alaska: Its History and Resources, Gold Fields, Routes, and Scenery.* Seattle: Lowman & Hanford, 1895.

Campbell, Robert. *Two Journals of Robert Campbell, 1808–1851.* Edited by John W. Todd, Jr. Seattle, 1958.

Cohen, Stan. *The Streets Were Paved with Gold: A Pictorial History of the Klondike Gold Rush.* Missoula, Mont.: Pictorial Histories, 1977.

Coutts, R. C. *Yukon: Places and Names.* Sidney, B.C.: Gray's, 1980.

Dictionary of the Chinook Jargon, or, Indian Trade Language of the North Pacific Coast. Seattle: Shorey, 1964, 1977.

Dyea and the Chilkoot Trail. Monograph distributed by Dyea, Ala., Society for Industrial Archaeology, fall 1990 study tour. Skagway, Ala.: Klondike Gold Rush National Historical Park, 20 August 1990.

Dyer, Addison Clark. "Diary: 14 March 1898 to 20 October 1899." Autograph manuscript. Personal collection of the author.

Emmons, George Thornton. *The Tlingit Indians.* Edited by Frederica de Laguna. Seattle: University of Washington Press, 1991.

Fountain, Andrew G., and Bruce H. Vaughn. *Yukon River: Freeze-Up Data (1883–1975).* Report prepared for the U.S. Department of the Interior, Geological Survey. Washington, D.C.: Government Printing Office, 1984.

Gates, Michael. *Gold at Fortymile Creek.* Vancouver: University of British Columbia Press, 1994.

Hacking, Norman. "The Great Klondike Shipping Boom, 1897–1898." *Sea Chest* 17 (September 1983): 18–37.

Hamilton, Walter R. *The Yukon Story.* Vancouver, B.C.: Mitchell, 1964.

Hamilton, William B. *The Macmillan Book of Canadian Place Names.* 2nd ed. Toronto: Macmillan, 1983.

Mathews, Richard. *The Yukon.* New York: Holt, Rinehart & Winston, 1968.

Mayer, Melanie J. *Klondike Women: True Tales of the 1897–1898 Gold Rush.* Athens: Ohio University Press, 1989.

Minter, Roy. *The White Pass: Gateway to the Klondike.* Fairbanks: University of Alaska Press, 1987.

Newman, Peter C. *Caesars of the Wilderness.* Vol. 2, *Company of Adventurers: The Story of the Hudson's Bay Company.* Markham, Ont.: Penguin, 1987. Reprint, New York: Penguin, 1988.

———. *Company of Adventurers.* Vol. 1, *Company of Adventurers: The Story of the Hudson's Bay Company.* Markham, Ont.: Penguin, 1985. Reprint, New York: Penguin, 1987.

———. *Empire of the Bay: An Illustrated History of the Hudson's Bay Company.* Markham, Ont.: Penguin, 1989.

Nichols, Jeannette Paddock. "Advertising and the Klondike." *Washington Historical Quarterly* 13 (January 1922): 20–26.

Orth, Donald J. *Dictionary of Alaska Place Names.* Washington, D.C.: Government Printing Office, 1967.

Phillips, James W. *Alaska-Yukon Place Names.* Seattle: University of Washington Press, 1973.

Pike, Warburton. *Through the Subarctic Forest.* London: Edward Arnold, 1896.

Probert, Thomas. *Lost Mines and Buried Treasure of the West.* Berkeley: University of California Press, 1977.

Satterfield, Archie. *Chilkoot Pass: The Most Famous Trail in the North.* Rev. ed. Anchorage: Alaska Northwest, 1978.

————. *Exploring the Yukon River.* Seattle: Mountaineers, 1979.

Schwatka, Frederick. *Along Alaska's Great River.* New York: Cassell & Company, 1885.

Stanley, William M. *A Mile of Gold: Strange Adventures on the Yukon.* Chicago: Laird & Lee, 1898.

"Townsite of Dyea." Unpublished monograph. Klondike Gold Rush National Historical Park, Skagway, Alaska, n.d.

Webb, Melody. *The Last Frontier: A History of the Yukon Basin of Canada and Alaska.* Albuquerque: University of New Mexico Press, 1985.

Wharton, David. *The Alaska Gold Rush.* Bloomington: Indiana University Press, 1972.

Winslow, Kathryn. *Big Pan-Out.* New York: W. W. Norton, 1951.

Wright, Allen A. *Prelude to Bonanza: The Discovery and Exploration of the Yukon.* Sidney, B.C.: Gray's, 1976.

Zaslow, Morris. *The Opening of the Canadian North, 1870–1914.* Toronto: McClelland & Stewart, 1971.

4. GENERAL REFERENCE

Beebe, Lucius. *Mr. Pullman's Elegant Palace Car.* Garden City, N.Y.: Doubleday, 1961.

Binns, Archie. *Northwest Gateway: The Story of the Port of Seattle.* Garden City, N.Y.: Doubleday, Doran, 1941.

Culin, Stewart. *The Gambling Games of the Chinese in America.* Publications of the University of Pennsylvania Series in Literature and Archaeology, vol. 1, no. 4, Philadelphia: 1891. Reprint, Las Vegas: Gambler's Book Club, 1972.

Hervey, John. "Life of John Myers O'Hara." [1939.] Typed manuscript, Special Collections, Newberry Library, Chicago.

Wilson, R. L. *The Colt Heritage: The Official History of Colt Firearms from 1836 to the Present.* New York: Simon & Schuster, 1979.

5. NEWSPAPERS

Daily Alaskan (Skagway), 1898–99, scattered issues.

Dyea Press, 1898, scattered weekly issues.

Dyea Trail, 1898, scattered weekly issues.

Klondike Nugget (Dawson City, Yukon).

New York Times.

Oakland Enquirer.

San Francisco Chronicle.

San Jose Daily Mercury, 1892, 1897–98.

Skaguay News, 1897–98, scattered weekly issues.

6. CALIFORNIA HISTORY AND GEOGRAPHY

Ford, Robert S. *Red Trains in the East Bay: The History of the Southern Pacific Transbay Train and Ferry System.* Glendale, Calif.: Interurbans, 1977.

Harlan, George H. *San Francisco Bay Ferryboats.* Berkeley, Calif.: Howell-North, 1967.

Historical Atlas Map of Santa Clara County, California. San Francisco: Thompson and West, 1876.

Jones, Herbert C. "Recollections of College Park in the 90's." *Trailblazer* 8 (summer 1968): n.p.

Payne, Stephen M. *Santa Clara County: Harvest of Change.* Northbridge, Calif.: Windsor, 1987.

Sawyer, Eugene T. *History of Santa Clara County.* Los Angeles: Historic Record Co., 1922.

Standard Time Schedules. San Francisco: Time Schedules Company, May 1897.

Sunshine, Fruit, and Flowers: Santa Clara County, California. San Jose: *San Jose Mercury,* 1896.

CPSIA information can be obtained at www.ICGtesting.com
Printed in the USA
LVOW03s0148090714

393416LV00020B/739/P